FURTHER ADVENTURES

Of

JAKE AND SANDY
(Sequel to WHOSE MONEY IS IT ANYWAY?)

I0553051

BY

WILLIAM H. CROFTON

This book is fictionalization. Names, characters, businesses, organizations, places, events and incidents are the product of the author's imagination or are used fictitiously.

DEDICATED
To Sylvia
And
To my family and friends.
I thank you for your support and encouragement.

SPECIAL THANKS
To Nancy Crofton for her valuable help in editing and to William H. Crofton III for his work on the cover.

INTRODUCTION

THE FURTHER ADVENTURES OF JAKE AND SANDY continues the story, which began with WHOSE MONEY IS IT ANYWAY? Published by Author House in 2010.

Jake with his dog Sandy move between their mountain cabin at Blackberry Inn outside of Weaverville, North Carolina and their beach cottage at Ocean Isle Beach, North Carolina.

After leaving the FBI Jake becomes a photographer, which places him in a variety of situations where his former FBI training helps him work with the local authorities to bring several criminals to justice and finally resolve his issues with John Wesley Williams.

Sandy, his dog, is always right there to assist and provide companionship. His friendship with Barbara and Susan continues to develop.

CHAPTER I

A NEW LIFE

JANUARY 16, 2003

Jake awoke with the sun in his eyes, but he was not in bed, he had spent the night in the recliner. He hesitated a moment to try to figure out if it was a dream. Had he really gotten a call from John that John Wesley Williams had escaped from the prison van during an accident while they were transporting him to Central Prison?

Jake had just gone through the ordeal of finding his parents and then sitting through the trials where the crooks who had turned his life upside down had been convicted and now this. Was trouble with these thugs going to start all over again?

It had been so peaceful sitting in his chair in his mountain cabin. He had already begun to miss

Barbara. Even though it was her job as an FBI agent that had brought them together he had really come to like her and he was sure the feelings were mutual.

He picked up the phone and dialed her number.

"Barbara, this is Jake. Did you hear about John Wesley Williams' escape?"

"Yes, I had a call from Malcolm and also from John. Seems like he is on the loose again, but he shouldn't be too hard to find. We will just stake out your cabin and when he comes to get you, we will nab him."

"That's not funny. I have not even had a chance to relax. Reckon I had better turn the alarm system back on."

"Have you thought about getting Jimbo back?"

"No, I really have not had time to think about much. I ended up sleeping in the chair last night after John called and I am a little stiff this morning. Keep me informed about what is happening. I miss you."

"I miss you too. Talk to you later."

A scratching at the door alerted Jake that Sandy wanted back in. He had left her outside all night. At least John Wesley Williams does not keep me from sleeping, he thought to himself. I need to get away for a while, and I should check out my beach place to see if everything is finished. Also it would be nice to catch some spots from the pier and

I could use some fresh ocean air. He also remembered he needed to settle up with Hazel and get the cottage set up to rent for its second season. He had put all this on the back burner while he was looking for his folks. With no one to answer to he could do whatever he wanted, within reason, of course. That settles it. I am off to the beach tomorrow.

CHAPTER 2

OCEAN ISLE BEACH

FRIDAY, JANUARY 17, 2003

The trip was long, but he and Sandy had enjoyed themselves. They had stopped several times to let her do her thing. She was a good traveler, riding sometimes with her head in Jake's lap and sometimes with her head out the window with her fur blowing in the breeze.

He couldn't see much difference in the island as he topped the bridge over the Inland Waterway and looked out over the brightly colored roofs and the beautiful blue water. It was January so there was not much activity going on. He stopped at the crest of the bridge and just took in all the beauty. The mountains he had left were beautiful, but there was something about the vastness of the ocean that brought you a little closer to your creator.

One of his friends had remarked that when you go over that bridge you get hungry and lazy. The lazy part had not hit him, but he was hungry. It was dusk and the brilliance of the sunset had passed. He stopped at the pier and bought a hamburger, fries and a Sprite. He and Sandy walked out on the deserted pier so he could eat his supper and take in what was left of a beautiful day.

Jake knew it was time to go when the chill of the January evening started getting to him. Overcoming his reluctance to leave the beach, he pried himself off the fisherman's perch and headed for his cottage. He knew he needed to get the heat and water operating so he could enjoy a comfortable night.

CHAPTER 3

LAZY DAYS AT THE BEACH

SATURDAY, MARCH 1, 2003

Jake and Sandy had enjoyed the isolation of a lonely beach for over a month. Eating, sleeping, walking on the beach and reading had consumed the beautiful days at the coast. John and Barbara had been busy and Jake's folks were away on a cruise so there was no one to interrupt his peaceful existence. Only Ken, the Buncolm County Sheriff, knew where he was and was looking after his mountain cabin for him. There was no word from anyone about the whereabouts of John Wesley Williams and Jake was just enjoying being alone. The solitude was akin to the time he had spent in the Smokies, but at least he had Sandy with him now and no schedules to keep.

Jake had left the shades up on purpose and the bright sun and the pounding of the waves at high tide woke him up even before Sandy could get to him. His thoughts went back to his meeting Susan when he had done the turtle photo shoot and he hoped she had not forgotten him. He certainly had not forgotten her. Her perfume still lingered in his mind and their short time together had meant a lot to him while he was trying to pull his life together after his wife's death and the disappearance of his mother and father. It was wonderful to have his mom and dad back in his life, but he dearly missed Jackie.

Sandy sensed he was awake and came in and put her paw on the bed, telling him it was time to get up and feed her. Jake patted her head and rolled out of bed and headed to the kitchen so he could feed Sandy.

He peered out the window, taking in the wide beach and pounding surf and the gently waving sea oats on the dunes. There was no one there as far as he could see in both directions. He could hardly wait to walk the beach looking for shells and just relax in the beauty of the seashore.

After breakfast he decided to take Sandy for a walk and go to the pier for a newspaper. Two ladies were out walking their dog in front of the motel and as Jake got nearer he heard both ladies screaming at the top of their voices and running back toward the motel. When they saw Jake they ran toward him.

"A dead man, a dead man!" shrieked the first one to reach him, pointing toward the field across from the motel.

"Are you sure he is dead?" Jake asked.

"Yes, Yes," cried the other lady who had just reached them with her dog in tow.

"Let's go take a look before we call 911. I am a former FBI agent," Jake said to both of them.

Jake walked across the road in the direction from which the ladies had come. The two ladies were right behind him chatting away in high-pitched nervous voices.

The man Jake saw was lying face down in the sand with a gun in his right hand. There was no question that he was dead, but Jake carefully checked for a pulse without disturbing the man or the surrounding area. When Jake bent over to check the pulse, Jake the nature photographer was gone and Jake the FBI agent was back. A piece of paper was crumpled in the man's left hand. There was a sunburn line and a depression where a ring had been. He had on a short sleeve shirt and green khaki pants. His hair was in a buzz cut and the shoelaces on his low top boots were untied.

"Call 911, but tell them not to panic, the man is already dead," Jake said to the one who was getting her cell phone out of her purse.

Jake glanced around the vacant lot and noticed no cars in the parking lot across the street or at the pier. How had the dead body gotten here?

Jake stayed away from the body. He did not want to contaminate what he had concluded was a crime scene. He could see two sets of footprints in the sand going toward the body that did not belong to the ladies. They were heavy and deep prints. He could also see lighter prints going away from the body. This indicated to him that two people had brought the body here.

Jake heard the sirens begin indicating that the 911 operator had alerted the authorities. Then there was a loud crash and the sound of metal against metal and one set of sirens ceased and then another was heard.

"Good grief. The patrol car has had a wreck," Jake said shaking his head in disbelief. "Hope no one was hurt."

The ladies finally picked up on what was happening and began chattering again.

In a few minutes Jake could see the patrolman running across the vacant lot just as the fire truck pulled up in front of the motel. Jake moved between the body and the oncoming deputy and suggested that he be careful and not disturb the scene because it was not really what it appeared to be.

"Who are you?' the deputy asked, showing his annoyance with someone telling him what to do.

"I'm Jake Johnson."

Before he could make any other explanation the officer exclaimed, "You are the former FBI man who bought 'Better Than Nutting.'"

"That's right," Jake said. "How did you know that?

"This is a small island and not much happens that all the permanent residents don't know about."

The deputy leaned over the body and checked

for a pulse. Finding none, he reached in the man's back pocket and extracted his wallet.

"Harry Farmer, Hillsville, Virginia," the deputy read from the driver's license and then activated his radio and reported to the chief what he had found.

The radio blasted forth, "I am about ten minutes away, call the coroner. I'll be right there."

The fire and rescue crew were now on the scene and the deputy asked them to rope off the area while he called the coroner.

Jake made sure they did not disturb the two sets of footprints that he had seen.

"The coroner will be here in about 30 minutes," the deputy said as he pocketed his phone.

The deputy came over to Jake and said, "I am Dan Spice. Chief Prevatte will be here in a few minutes. He had gone into Shallotte."

One of the firemen came over and jokingly said, "The chief is going to have your hide for wrecking that new squad car."

"I know, I know. I got excited and ran the red light and clipped that Plum Rite plumbing truck that was going through the intersection. The chief will not let me live that down. I'll be washing the squad cars the rest of the time I am on the force."

Jake asked the group standing around if anyone knew Mr. Farmer. Everyone shook their heads and started talking among themselves again. While waiting for the chief and the coroner, Jake decided to walk over to the motels to check to see if he was a guest at either one.

When Jake went in the office, the clerk was standing at the window peering at the crowd across the street.

"What's happening?' the clerk asked in an excited tone.

"The two ladies found a dead man lying over there in the vacant lot. His name is Harry Farmer from Hillsville, Virginia according to his driver's license. Is he by chance staying at this motel?"

The clerk quickly searched his records and shook his head.

"No one here by that name."

"Would you mind calling the other motels in the area and asking if they have a Harry Farmer registered."

Without questioning Jake's authority to do this, the clerk quickly called the other motels on the island, but none of them had anyone with the last name Farmer registered.

Jake thanked him and went out the door and across the street just as the chief was pulling up with his lights flashing. Jake introduced himself to the chief as they walked across the lot toward the crowd that had now gathered.

"I remember you from Susan's party. Did you ever find out why they called it Frog More Stew? Sometime when we have some time I'll tell you about it. I later found out you are former FBI."

"No I never found out about the stew and would like to know and second being a former FBI agent does not give me any brownie points."

The chief seemed to be impressed that Jake

was a former FBI agent.

"I checked with the motels in the area and no one had him listed as a guest. He gives the appearance he might be military," Jake told the chief, apologizing for his actions, well knowing that local law enforcement officials do not take kindly to getting advice from other people, especially someone formerly with the FBI.

"I know that I shouldn't get involved, but my instincts just took over. I reckon you cannot get the FBI out of the man even if the man is not in the FBI any more."

"Appreciate your help," the chief said as he patted Jake on the back and noticed that Jake had a revolver stuck in his back belt under his shirt.

"You do have a permit for that thing, don't you?"

"Sure do."

"Stick around I would like to talk to you some more. Here comes the coroner. Will be glad to get the body moved and these people out of here."

Even though it was January, Jake was getting pretty warm standing out there in the morning sun. He then realized that he had not seen Sandy in a while. Looking around, he saw some little kids sitting down beside her as she lay in the sand. They were enjoying petting her, but not as much as she was enjoying getting petted. When she saw Jake she got up and wandered over to him and nudged his leg.

"Deputy, take a statement from the two ladies

who found the body and from Jake. Then get the camera and take some pictures so we can get this body out of here.

The deputy left to go to his car to get his forms and the camera.

"Can you determine the cause and time of death?" the Chief asked the coroner.

"Looks like it might have been about one or two o'clock this morning, and it looks like one gunshot to the head, but I'll know better when I get him back to the office. Here is the piece of paper that was in his hand."

The chief carefully took the note and read it out loud in a muffled voice.

"Honey, I love you and am sorry about this, but it is for the best. Forgive me. Love Harry."

Jake was standing close enough to the chief that he could hear what he read and could see the carefully written note.

"Looks like it could be a suicide," the chief said to no one in particular.

After turning and seeing Jake right there the Chief said, "What do you think, Mr. FBI man? Is it a suicide?"

Jake sensed the sarcasm in his voice, but decided to go on and say what he was thinking. "Well Chief, if I agree with you, we will both be wrong. The note seems a little strange, and there is no blood and the two sets of footprints makes me wonder if he really shot himself here or if someone killed him somewhere else and brought him here."

"Is that right about the blood, Julius?" the chief

asked the coroner.

"He is right about that. If he had been shot here, there would have been a pool of blood right where he was lying."

"As soon as Dan gets back I'll get him to take some more pictures of the body and also of the footprints. Wonder if we should try to take a cast of the prints," the chief said to no one in particular as he raised his cap and scratched his head.

"Might be a good idea," Jake said. "The lab boys might be able to find some distinguishing marks that might make a difference in making the case if it turns out to be a murder."

The deputy returned with a notepad and a camera and told the chief he had gotten statements from the ladies.

"Chief, what do you want pictures of? " Dan asked.

"Anything that looks out of place, but especially of the body and the footprints leading to and from the body. Put a marker down so we can identify each different picture you take. Jake, you mind showing him what he should be shooting about the footprints? Don't forget to get some cast of the footprints."

"OK Chief."

"Julius, as soon as you finish with the body let's get it out of here so you can try to get us some more information about what happened."

"Just a few more minutes, Chief, I am not as fast as those TV people."

A reporter from the Brunswick Beacon approached the chief and said, "Chief, can I ask you some questions about this?"

"Julie, you know I'll give you all the information I can, but let me get this area cleared out first."

"OK Chief," and she walked off with her camera taking in the whole situation. She got pictures of the body and the surrounding area and the crowd that had gathered and the chief talking to the coroner and Jake and the deputy taking pictures of the footprints. The pictures would be splashed all over the next paper that came out. A suspicious death did not happen often in the small beach community and would be the talk of the surrounding area,

The coroner finished and the body was taken away. The crowd began to disperse as the emergency vehicles left the scene. Jake, the chief, the deputy and the reporter were the only ones left.

Jake watched as Dan got out his casting kit and laid the form over a set of the footprints.

"Chief, the can of stuff in the casting kit is all dried up. What should I do?"

"Darn it, Dan, I told you to keep everything up to date so we would have it when we need it."

Jake, hearing the hostility in the chief's voice, whispered in Dan's ear, "Get a can of heavy duty hair spray and that will do just fine."

Dan whispered to Jake, " I owe you one," and then hollered to the chief as he was walking away, "That's OK Chief, I got it covered."

"Get back to the station as soon as you can

Dan, we have a lot of work to do. Jake, are you going to be around for a while?"

"Don't have any definite plans so I'll be around for a couple of days."

"I'll be in touch. Thanks for your help. Come on Julie, let's go to my office and I'll tell you what I know that you can print now."

Jake was glad that the chief wanted to go it alone. He was out of this kind of business and glad to just be able to relax and enjoy the beach. In the back of his mind he was wondering what had happened about John Wesley Williams. Had the authorities caught him yet? Would he be coming to look for Jake as he had threatened at the trial?

"Come on Sandy, let's go get our paper and get back to the cottage. I bet you are hungry again."

At the pier the attendant started asking Jake a lot of questions about what had been going on. Jake asked him how long had he been there and if he was there last night.

"No, this time of year with no fishermen I close early in the evening after the fellows have shot their pool games and eaten their hamburgers."

"Do you have a security camera?" Jake asked.

"No, we are not that sophisticated. This time of year there is nothing here anyone wants and in the season we are here all the time so there is no need for cameras."

"Is there a beach cam?"

"Yeah, Cooke Realty has one, but it is pointed at the beach and wouldn't take in anything in that parking lot or in the streets. The motel does not have any cameras either. The only eyes that might be open at that hour might be those of Dell Williams. I understand he has a hard time sleeping these days."

"Dell is in the brick house on the hill?" Jake asked.

"Yeah, he owned the whole island at one time and picked the highest point on the island to build his house. Not much traffic here this time of year; he might be the best bet of anyone seeing anything. Say, you are that FBI man aren't you? That is why you are asking so many questions."

"Yes, I am Jake Johnson. I am out of the FBI business, but I was just curious if there was anything I might help the chief with. I am just enjoying Better Than Nuttin," Jake said as he puts out his hand to shake hands.

"I'm Calvin Britt, I just work here. Ron Simpson owns the place, but he is away in Florida for a while."

Jake called Sandy, as she was busy licking something off the floor. Jake told Calvin that he had better get back to the cottage.

Back at the cottage, sitting on the deck in a rocking chair in the warm sun, Jake read the paper, but his mind was still racing around all that he had seen and heard in the past few hours.

He picked up his binoculars as he saw a sailboat on the horizon. Someone decided to take a shortcut rather than stay in the Inland Water Way. It certainly was a perfect day for it as the ocean was as calm as a millpond.

Jake put down the binoculars and lay his head back and relaxed in the old gray rocking chair. In a few minutes he was fast asleep.

For the next few days Jake and Sandy just enjoyed walking on the beach and sitting on the porch eating and getting lazier all the time.

CHAPTER 4

VISITORS

SATURDAY, MARCH 15, 2003

Jake was sitting on the porch finishing his lunch and watching the pelicans dive for their food. Sandy had her head stuck through the railings taking advantage of every bit of the cool breeze and warm sunshine.

Suddenly, Sandy perked up her ears and quickly pulled her head from between the railings and gave a quick low bark. Jake then realized that she had heard someone knocking on his door. Looking inside the cottage he could see a man and a woman standing on his street-side porch. He went into the cottage and opened the outer door, but did not open the storm door.

The man said, "Mr. Johnson, may my wife and I come in to talk to you? I am Harry Farmer, senior."

It took Jake just a minute to realize that Mr. Farmer senior was the father of the dead man who had been found in the sand dune.

"Yes sir. Just a minute, let me unlock the door."

As Jake opened the door, he put out his hand to shake Mr. Farmer's hand.

"This is my wife, Betty," Mr. Farmer said as he put his hand on her waist and ushered her into the room.

"I am very sorry about your son. What can I do for you?"

"We understand that you were there when the body was found and that you might have a little different slant on what happened than the chief does. He has not ruled out suicide."

"I have not talked to him in a few days so I am not sure what he has concluded, but from what I saw I would have ruled out suicide. Has the military or the FBI gotten in on the case yet?"

"Not sure about the FBI. We have been contacted by the military, but they wouldn't say much about it. They just asked a lot of questions, but we couldn't tell what they were thinking."

"Who does 'honey' refer to in the note? Was he married? I did not see a wedding band on his hand." Jake asked.

"We do not have a clue. He had a girl in high school, but when he went into the military it was not long before she got married to someone else. As far as we know he did not have a close girlfriend at the time. He left his class ring at home when he joined the service," Mrs. Farmer said in a very soft voice.

"Do you have any idea whether your son was having problems with anyone?"

"No. We have not seen much of him since he joined the military. He went off to basic training and then was shipped to Iraq, so we have not had a lot of contact with him for about the last couple of years. He did write regularly when he could, but his letters were pretty general, just trying to assure us that he was all right. When he came home after basic training for a few days he slept most of the time. He managed to see some of his buddies who were still around. He was a good boy and we were a pretty close family," Mrs. Farmer said as she wiped a tear from her eye.

Jake could feel the hurt in her heart because he had been through losing a loved one when Jackie had been killed and when he thought his folks were dead. It must be doubly hard when you lose a child because you expect them to outlive you.

Sandy had come over and put her paw on Mrs. Farmer's leg as she was talking as if to say, everything is going to be all right.

"I am not sure how I can help. The local law officials do not like outsiders prying into their cases."

"We are convinced it was not a suicide and we want to know what really happened. We will be glad to pay you for your time and trouble. Our son had a large insurance policy that we had purchased for him when he was a kid and they will not pay if it is ruled a suicide. Of course, it is not the money we are concerned with. We are retired, but we did well in our business and money is not a problem. Harry came to us late in life, but we loved him so much." Mr. Farmer's eyes began to water.

Sandy must have felt their grief because she was now at Mr. Farmer's feet lying with her head on his shoe as he was talking.

Jake liked these people from the beginning, and though he was reluctant to get involved, but he knew it was the right thing to do. He did not have any pressing matters now and really no real reason not to see what he could find out for them. It would also take his mind off John Wesley Williams and what was happening with him. There was really no question that Jake would try to help the Farmers gain peace of mind about the tragedy that had become a part of their lives.

"I am not going to make any promises, but i'll look into it for you and see what we can find out. Give me a list of his friends and any information about his military service. You can send it General Delivery here at Ocean Isle Beach. I really live utside Asheville, but I need to get a Post Office box down here and I'll give you that information as soon as I get it. Here is my cell phone number where I can be reached no matter if I am here or in Weaverville. Can I get you something to eat or drink?"

"No thank you, we must go, we have a long drive back to Hillsville," Mr. Farmer replied as he reached down and patted Sandy who was still lying on his feet. He handed Jake a business card with his contact information.

"I'll be in touch," Jake said as he walked to the door with them and gave Mrs. Farmer a hug and shook Mr. Farmer's hand with both of his.

Jake watched as they got in their car and drove away. He felt their loss as he did his own when Jackie was shot and killed in the convenience store. He hoped he could get some answers for them that would make losing Harry a little easier for them.

CHAPTER 5

TALK WITH THE CHIEF

MONDAY, MARCH 31, 2003 A.M.

It had been over a week since the body was found and the chief had not contacted Jake. Jake needed some more information if he was going to try to help the Farmers.

Jake decided it was time to go talk to the chief. He picked up his hat and coat and headed for the door, saying to Sandy on the way out, " Stay, I'll be back in a little while." She looked a little forlorn, but laid her head back on her paw and stared at him as he went out the door.

The breeze was brisk, but the March sunshine was still warm as Jake walked down the steps and into the street and headed toward the city hall where the police chief had his office.

As Jake entered the police station he was

greeted by the deputy, "Hello Jake."

"Dan, how are you doing, you haven't wrecked any more patrol cars have you? Jake asked with a sly grin on his face."

"You don't have to bring that up," Dan said with a scowl on his face.

"Is the chief in?"

"Sure is, just go on back."

Jake knocked on the door as he entered and the chief looked up and got out of his chair to shake Jake's hand.

"Been meaning to call you. Understand you had some visitors the other afternoon. Hope you did not mind."

"No, they are real nice people and I really feel for them. I know how it is to lose someone you love. It must be doubly hard to lose your child."

"They seemed to want more answers than we could give them right now and I thought you might be able to help us bridge that gap."

"Anything else turn up?"

"We have a copy of the coroner's report. Would you like to have a copy?"

Knowing the answer was going to be yes, the chief pushed the intercom button and asked Dan to bring Jake a copy of the report.

Jake took a chair and when Dan brought the report to him he began reading it.

"Want a cup of coffee?" the chief asked Jake as he left the room.

"No thanks, I'm fine," Jake said as he intently studied the three-page report.

"Looks like this might rule out suicide," Jake said to the chief as he reentered the room with a steaming cup of coffee in his hand.

"Why so?"

"The fact that the fingers and thumbs on both hands were broken would suggest to me that he would have a hard time shooting himself with a pistol."

"Yeah, I was wondering if you would pick up on that, but all along you have thought it was not a suicide. If someone did kill him, why would they pick Ocean Isle Beach to dispose of the body?"

"That is not as important as why was he killed?"

"A JAG team from Camp Jackson in South Carolina where he was stationed is coming back this afternoon. Would you like to sit in on the meeting?

"Yes, I would, but I am a little surprised that you would ask me to."

"To be honest I got a call from your old boss, Malcolm, saying they were putting a team together to come down since it was more than just a local homicide and he suggested I get you involved if I could. He must think a lot of you even though you are not with the bureau any longer."

"Well, since we are being honest, I told the Farmers that they should give him a call, and evidently they did. Malcolm is a good agent and also a good friend. He was there for me when Jackie was killed and my parents went missing."

"Jake, I like your style. You are not pushy, but seem interested in helping without getting in the way. The JAG officers are to be here about two this afternoon. Can you join us?"

"Sure, if it is all right with you. You know that the Farmers did hire me to try to help find out what really happened?"

"I guessed as much and that is all right with me. You might be able to keep the feds from completely taking over the case. I am up for reelection and this case might be a help in getting elected again if I can show that I can work with all sides and still get the case solved on our own turf."

"Sounds like a plan to me. I'll stay in the background, but would appreciate being kept in the loop. I have to go back to the house to take care of Sandy, but I'll be back here at two."

Walking back home, Jake used his cell phone to call John, his old FBI partner.

"Where are you calling from?" John asked as he answered the phone and recognized Jake's phone number on his display.

"I'm at Ocean Isle Beach taking in a beautiful April day here in North Carolina."

"Go ahead, make up my bed, Malcolm has just informed me that I am on my way down. Seems like you are in the middle of a homicide."

"Yeah it looks that way. The JAG crew from Fort Jackson is going to be here this afternoon and the chief has asked me to sit in on the meeting. He is making me an official, unofficial, member of his task force. My job, in so many words, is to keep you people at bay so he can grab all the limelight and get himself re-elected. My purpose is to try to help the Farmers work through the death of their son."

"Sounds like you have your fingers already deep in the pie. By the way, we have not a single clue what has happened to John Wesley Williams. He has dropped completely off the radar."

"Looks like you are going to use me for bait again, huh? Why don't you suggest that Barbara come with you? You both can stay with me and save the government some money. When are you going to be here?"

"I was going to let her surprise you. She is coming down and we will be there tomorrow. We are flying into Myrtle Beach and picking up a car at the field office. Should be there late in the afternoon. I want some of that Frog More Stew I have heard you talk about. Act surprised when you see us."

"In that case I'll let you make up your own beds then. Will be good to see you both. Talk to you later."

Jake made a mental note that he had to go to Wal-Mart in Shallotte and pick up another set of sheets, something suitable for Barbara.

Sandy greeted him at the door, but did not linger as she went down the stairs to take care of her business. Jake thought that he needed a pet door, but wondered if that would be wise. He did not want his summertime renters to think they could have pets at his place. Sandy was more than a pet so he would be more careful to look after her needs.

CHAPTER 6

MEET THE JAG BOYS

MARCH 31, 2010 P.M.

As Jake and Sandy entered the police station there were two guys and a girl in plain clothes, but with the look of military all over them, getting out of a car in the parking lot. Jake chuckled to himself as he thought that they did not look a bit like Jethro Gibbs and his crew from the NCIS television show.

"The chief is in the conference room in the back. Go on back. Tell the chief that our visitors are here. I'll bring them back," Dan said to Jake as he entered the front door.

Jake went down the hall and found the chief moving more chairs into the conference room.

"There are three of them, Chief. Dan is bringing them back," Jake said as he picked up a chair and placed it at the table.

"I understand your Fed friends will be here later this week. This room is going to get a little crowded," the chief said with a little frown on his face.

Before Jake could say anything, Dan entered the room followed by the JAG officers. He introduced them to the chief.

"Special Agent Coleman, this is Chief Prevatte," Dan said as the two shook hands.

"Chief Prevatte, this is Special agent Fish and Special Agent Bradley."

Without any other explanation the chief introduced Jake to the three agents and they all took seats at the table. The three agents took up one side of the table and the chief, Dan and Jake faced them on the other side of the table. Sandy staked out her place beside Jake at the end of the table.

"Anyone care for coffee before we get started?" the chief asked.

Agent Coleman said yes, but everyone else declined. The chief pushed the intercom and said, "Dorothy, would you please bring in two cups of coffee."

Jake did not realize that there was anyone else in the office and was surprised when the chief called someone to bring in the coffee. In a minute a nice looking brunette in a police uniform with a good beach tan came in carrying a tray with the coffee, cream, and sugar.

"This is Dorothy Townsend," the chief said to everyone with no other explanation.

Jake glanced at her left hand as she smiled at

him.   No ring, Jake thought to himself as he remembered meeting her at Susan's party last year. He had been a little lonely since Barbara had moved back to the DC area and having another friend wouldn't be bad. Could he really juggle three women?

"We thank you for your time, Chief, and hope we can work together to resolve this case. We will provide you all the information   we can and expect you to do the same for us. Could we ask what is Jake's role is in all this? "

Chief Prevatte waited a minute before he answered Agent Coleman's question, wondering just what he ought to say.

"Jake is a resident of the island and he was there when the body was found. He is a former FBI agent and was a help in the initial investigation. The team of FBI agents coming down are friends of his, and Malcolm, his old boss, says it would be helpful to have Jake kept in the loop. The parents of the deceased have also talked to Jake about the investigation."

Jake felt a little uncomfortable as the three agents gave him the once over, but he did not feel the necessity to add anything to what the chief had told them. He realized he was on thin ice as an outsider with three different law enforcement agencies working together, clogging the playing field with their rival agendas.

"Jake, glad you are willing to help. As an aside, have they been able to find John Wesley

Williams yet?"

Jake was surprised that they had to ask him this and he stammered out a weak, "Not yet." Then he decided to be bolder and asked, "How do you know about Mr. Williams?"

"Malcolm told us when he let us know he was sending a team down. He thinks a lot of you and believes you can be of assistance in this case."

Jake turned a little red as he was embarrassed by this, but managed to say, "Thank you." He wondered why Agent Coleman asked the chief what his role was since he already knew the answer.

"Now back to the business at hand," Agent Coleman said as he pulled a file folder out of his brief case.

"Sergeant Farmer was stationed at Fort Jackson and was working in the Paymaster's office. He was a courier with the responsibility of transporting large sums of money between bases. Most if it was done electronically, but occasionally it was necessary to actually transport cash. He had a high clearance rating and had been checked out thoroughly. We believe his honesty and loyalty to his job are what might have gotten him killed. We surmised from the coroner's report that the broken fingers might have been a form of torture to try to get information out of him. We're still trying to determine if there actually was a theft involved with the death or whether they were trying to get information for future use. From your description of the crime scene we know that there were at least two people involved. Their feeble attempt to make it look like suicide shows they are not the shiniest apples on the tree."

"Do we have any idea what he was doing at Ocean Isle and why he was he in civilian clothes?" the chief asked.

"We have been tracking his movements and he was actually signed out for a trip from Jackson to Fort Bragg. Since it is off season the people might have thought that the beach would be a deserted place to leave him," Agent Bradley interjected into the conversation.

"He was wearing civilian clothes because it is sometimes done to make the courier less conspicuous when they are traveling between bases," Agent Fish contributed.

"It is a long shot, but these goons might have been staying down here because it would be a place they could bring him to torture him without very many people being around," Jake said to the group.

"It will not be too hard to find out about all the house rentals and motel guests this time of year. We can also check about any break-ins, but that will be a little hard until the owners or maintenance people check out their properties," the chief said.

"At this point we do not have any leads on who might have done this so we will be tracking down every scrap of evidence. The body has been transferred to the lab where they are looking for any latent evidence that can give us a clue where to turn. We would also like to send the footprint impressions you have to the lab for further analysis."

The chief turned to Deputy Spice and said, "Dan, see to it that they get the impressions before they leave. Let them look at any crime scene photos to see if there is anything they can use."

"It's going to seem like a lot of duplication between the three agencies, but if we each stake out our areas of expertise and pool our resources, we can get to the bottom of this. We will keep the FBI informed and our bosses will see that we don't kill each other," Agent Coleman said.

"Can we definitely say it was not a suicide and let the family move on from this premise? Even though it is hard to lose a son they will feel better knowing he did not take his own life. Will they also be able to realize some compensation from their insurance if it is not a suicide?" Jake asked the group.

"Yes, we can get a death certificate issued that will clear out any road blocks and release the body for burial in the very near future. The lab is about finished with it. Hopefully this will ease the pain a little for the family," Agent Coleman replied.

"Unless someone else has questions or something to add, I believe we are finished. Dan will get the information you requested," the chief said to the group

The group pushed back from the table, picked up their papers and prepared to leave without much small talk.

Jake thought that the meeting went pretty well without much of a spitting contest. Everyone seemed content with their place in the investigation. He was the only one who did not have a superior to answer to, but he was delighted that the Farmers could be brought up to date on the findings so far. He wondered if they would be interested in having him pursue it any farther.

On the way out Jake stopped to speak to Ms. Townsend, but she was not anywhere to be found.

CHAPTER 7

JAKE THE SCAMEE

APRIL 1, 2003

It had started raining early in the morning, so Jake decided it would be a good time to go to Wilmington to do some shopping. He needed some more bed sheets and other things for the upcoming visit of John and Barbara. The weather had broken and now it was a beautiful day. He had finished his main shopping and decided to stop at the big grocery store on Highway 17 before heading back to Ocean Isle. It was one place that he could find some dog food that Sandy really liked.

As he finished putting his groceries in his truck a man approached him with a note in his hand and asked if he would help him. He said he needed to find these apartments as he had rented one for $300 a night from a Christian woman he had met in town. When Jake questioned him about the price he began telling a story about being from South Africa and having received a letter about the death of his brother.

He claimed his brother had worked for Brown and Root Construction Company and had died from a fall from a tall building. Since he was the only living relative, the lawyer had contacted him to come to Wilmington to settle the estate. He was a merchant seaman and worked out of Baltimore, but had come into Wilmington and was trying to find a place to stay for a couple of months while he settled his brother's estate.

He told Jake that he had met a Christian lady downtown who had befriended him and told him she had a place where he could stay while he was in town.

He pulled out a big roll of bills, started peeling off $100 bills and told Jake that he would be glad to pay him if he could help him.

"What's your name? I'm Jake."

"My name is Caprisha, which means fanciful, but they call me Capri."

Jake shook Capri's hand. "Put away that money. I don't want your money and besides, the wrong people would kill you for that roll of bills. Why are you carrying all that money, anyway?"

"My boss told me not to trust banks in the US because checks bounce all the time over here. That is why I have $250,000 on me now."

Jake was beginning to become suspicious of

this story, but his detective background made him want to see where it would lead.

"Get in my truck and I'll see if I can help you find those apartments since you have already paid that outrageous price for a night. That is more like a month's rent. How did you get out here to the shopping center?"

"The nice Christian lady who rented me the apartment got a taxi for me to come out here to the Rite Aid Drug Store, but when we got here there was no drug store. I paid the cab driver $200 to wait for me while I went into a store to find out where the drug store was and he went off and left me."

Knowing taxi drivers like he did from Washington, D.C. Jake knew that the taxi driver certainly would have stayed around if he had thought there might be more money like that being flashed around.

"We'll find the store," Jake said as he started the truck.

Jake pulled out of the parking space and then quickly backed up and cut the motor off.

"Give me a minute, I just realized that I have forgotten to get something in the store. I'll be right back."

Jake got out of the truck and went into the store. When he was out of sight, he dialed 911 on his cell phone and when the operator answered Jake said, "I am Jake Johnson. This is not an emergency, but I am in the middle of a scam and would like to leave my cell phone on so you can hear what is happening. I am at the shopping center on Highway 17. I am in a green Ford pick-up, license plate VPC 9867. Will be heading into Wilmington toward Market Street. Do not have time for any further explanation at this time. Please do not have a marked car anywhere around my truck. I'll let you know when to come if you will listen on the phone. If you want to check me out call 330-679-0003 and ask for Malcolm."

Jake quickly picked up a bag of dog food, paid the cashier and went back to the truck. He threw the dog food into the rear of the truck and climbed into the driver's seat.

"Sorry about that, but now we are ready to go. Let's see if we can find those apartments for you, but first you say you need to go to a Rite Aid Drug Store."

"Yes. The Christian lady told me that she would meet me there, but she didn't tell me which one. I thought the cab driver was going to take me there, but all he wanted was my money. I'll pay you if you can help me. I have $250,000 from the settlement, I can pay."

"Keep your money. If you keep flashing that much money around, someone is going to knock you in the head and take it all away from you. Why did you not get a check for the settlement?"

"My boss man tells me that checks are no good in America. Bad checks are everywhere. People cheat you with bad checks."

"The bank would have given you a cashier's

check that would have been good anywhere."

"No! No! Cannot use a bank. They will not give me my money back if I put it in there. They will not let me go into the bank. They sic the dogs on me and hit me with sticks. I am afraid of banks. No one, but Jews and Chinamen can use banks."

"That might be the way it is in South Africa, but not in America."

Jake made a couple of turns and figured out he was being followed by a small black Honda sedan.

"Do you know anyone here in America?" Jake asked.

"No, mister Jake, just you and the Christian lady whose name is on the piece of paper. Have only been here one day. Just off the boat."

Someone is following us around, Jake thought. Wonder what you have up your sleeve?

"We will be coming to the Rite Aid Drug store in just a minute. Why do you need to go there?

"The Christian Lady told me they would know where the apartments were."

"There are several Rite Aid Drug Stores. How did she know you would get to the right one?"

"The taxi driver was to take me to it, but then he left me where there was not a store."

Jake turned off Market Street into the parking lot of a drug store, but it was not a Rite Aid store.

Here we are, but I have taken you to the wrong place, I thought this was a Rite Aid.

Jake watched as a black sedan pulled into the parking lot and a man got out and started walking toward Jake's truck. He was holding a cell phone to his ear. As he walked past the truck, Capri said, "Ask that man, he might know where the Rite Aid Store is?"

Jake rolled down the window and called the man over to the truck.

Capri took out his roll of bills and said to the man, "If you help me find these apartments, I'll pay you."

He pulled off a hundred dollar bill and tried to hand it to the man.

"Sir, put your money away. If you flash money like that some of these boys with their pants down to their ankles will knock you in the head and take your money."

"Can you help me?"

Looking at Jake the man said, "What is your name? I'm Ben."

"Jake."

"Mister Jake have you got time to help this man? He needs to get his money in a bank. He shouldn't be carrying a wad of bills like that, he is going to get himself killed."

"That is what I have been telling him."

"Mr. Jake, can I come get in your truck and let's talk some sense into this man's head."

"Sure Ben," Jake said, as he reached into the pocket on the truck door and put his hand on his gun while the man got into the truck.

"No bank! No bank! They have dogs in the bank, they will bite me! The men there will hit me with sticks! They won't let me have my money back! No bank!"

"This is the United States, they will not do that to you here," the man said loudly to Capri.

"No one, but Jews and Chinamen can use banks. They will keep my money."

"Mr. Jake, tell this man that they will not do this to him here and the bank is the best place for his money. Do you have an account in a bank, Mr. Jake?"

"Yes I do." Jake answered.

"See Capri, everyone here uses banks. You can get your money any time you want to by writing a check or using a bank card."

"What's a bank card?" Capri asked Ben.

"Show him your bank card, Mr. Jake. Let him see how easy it is to get your money out of the bank."

"Someone take and use my card and get my money. That is not safe place for my money."

"They would have to have the code to punch in to get your money. Only you have that code."

Jake was beginning to wonder where this was going. He knew that they wanted money from him, but he did not know yet exactly what they had in mind. He hoped the 911 operator was still listening. He would like to have these fellows make their move so the police could move in. He was glad he did not have any ice cream in his grocery bags.

"Mr. Jake, how can we convince this man that he can trust the banks and they will not keep his money? Let's take him to a bank and show him how it works."

"No, no. No," Capri yelled as he started to open the truck door.

Ben grabbed his arm and said, "Wait, don't get out, we are going to help you."

Jake knew that he had to be careful what he said. He did not want anything he said to be construed to be entrapment. Jake hesitated a few minutes and then said, "Ben, how do you think we can help him?" This had gone on long enough; Jake wanted them to make their move. He had no idea if the police were still listening in or not.

Finally Capri calmed down and said, "You fellows have money in the bank. Can you get it out any time you want to?"

"Sure," Ben answered very quickly.

"Then show me," Capri shot right back."

"Come on Mr. Jake, let's go draw some money out and show Capri he can get his money any time he wants to. Come on Capri, we will show you how to get money out."

"No I am not going near that bank until I know it is safe. I'll stay right here and wait for you to come back with the money. I don't believe they will give you any money. Let me see how much money you have on you so I'll know that you got it out of the bank."

Ben opened his wallet and showed Capri that he had $150.

After taking his wallet out and putting it into his

right hand, Jake put his left hand on his gun just in case they decided to try to take his money from him. Jake opened his wallet and showed Capri that he had $246.

"Each of you bring back $1,000 and I'll know that you got it out of the bank."

"Come on Mr. Jake, let's go get the money. I'll write a check and you can use your ATM card so Capri can see both ways that he can get his money out of the bank."

The two men got out of the truck and left Capri sitting on the front seat. Jake checked his pocket to be sure he had his keys. They walked from the parking lot into the bank lot where the ATM machine was located.

As they walked toward the ATM machine, Ben began to talk to Jake.

"Mr. Jake, I am embarrassed. I want to help this man get his money in a safe place before someone hits him in the head and takes it, but I do not have a thousand dollars in the bank right now. Can you take out two thousand and let us pretend that a thousand of it is mine and I'll get it back to you as soon as we get Capri to deposit his money?"

Jake saw where this was going, but decided to play along and said to Ben, " Yeah, I reckon I can do that. The money is not going out of my sight."

"No sir, I'll give it right back to you. We can put each thousand in one of the deposit envelopes so we can show Capri that we both got money out," said Ben as he took two envelopes out of the deposit drawer.

"When you write your check inside the bank you can give it to me and I'll hold it until I get my money back from you," Jake said looking Ben straight in the eye.

Ben started to hesitate, but saw how serious Jake was and said, "Sure, that is a good idea."

"You go ahead Mr. Jake and get out the two thousand and I'll go inside and pretend to cash a check."

Jake took his ATM card out and put it into the machine and punched in his code. The machine clicked away and punched out five hundred dollars and Jake put it into one of the envelopes Ben had given him. He did this three more times and then put one thousand in one envelope and a thousand in another envelope. Jake took his pocketknife and with the smallest blade he marked one envelope with one prick and the other envelope with two pricks much like you would mark a deck of cards. By this time Ben was out of the bank. Jake handed Ben the envelope with the two pricks and got the check from Ben and they walked back toward the truck.

"This should ease his mind and show him how easy it is to get money out and that the people in the bank will not harm him." Ben said slapping Jake on the back.

When they got back in the truck Ben handed Capri his envelope and Capri thumbed through the bills and then sealed up the envelope and handed it back to Ben. Jake handed his envelope to Capri who looked at the money and then sealed up the envelope.

Just as Capri was going to hand the envelope back to Jake, He let out a big sneeze and dropped the envelopes on the floor, distracting Jake from what was happening.

When Ben handed Jake the envelope, Jake carefully checked it without letting on what he was doing and found that it had no prick marks. He knew that they had somehow exchanged the envelopes.

"That should satisfy you, Capri. Let's go deposit that wad of money you have so I can feel comfortable about you not getting killed," Ben said to Capri.

"Let's go in the bank and do this. I have my passport right here," Capri said.

The three men got out of the truck and went into the bank. Once inside, Capri said, " Mr. Jake you wait for us out here in the lobby while Ben and I go in and talk to the manager. I want to see that he will treat two black men fairly."

"That's OK with me," Jake said as he took a seat.

Ben handed Jake his envelope and asked him to hold it for him while they were in the manager's office.

Jake quickly noticed that this envelope did not have his marking on it either.

Ben and Capri were ushered into the manager's office and as they closed the door Jake talked into his cell phone.

"911, they are about to close the deal. Have your unmarked patrol car outside the bank and when I say, 'Don't you fellows want to get some ice cream?' and raise my hand, that will be your cue to make the arrest."

In a moment Capri and Ben came out of the office and shook the manager's hand. Capri had some papers in his hand. As they walked out of the bank, Ben said to Jake, "Well, it is all done. Capri does not want to bother you any more. The manager called us a cab and I am going to take Capri to his new apartment."

Capri took a hundred dollar bill out of his pocket and handed it to Jake, saying, "Mr. Jake, you have been so kind to me and have tried to help me and I want you to have this for your troubles."

"Thank you very much. Let's go get some ice cream to celebrate," Jake said as he raised his hand as a signal for the police, hoping that they were going to be there.

Jake saw a man and a woman get out of a car in the parking lot and walk toward them. They had the air of the police about them, but he was not sure. As they approached, the male officer took his badge out and said to the group, "What is going on here?"

Jake said, "I am Jake Johnson and I am the one you have been listening to. These two fellows have just conned me out of two thousand dollars."

"What is he talking about?" Ben said to the officers.

"Let's see some identification," the officer said to Ben and Capri.

They pulled out their wallets and handed their driver's licenses to the officer.

"James Washington from Richmond, Virginia. I thought your name was Capri?"

Turning to the other man, the officer said, "Ben Turlington also from Richmond."

"You fellows are a long way from home. Let me go check this out."

"Search them and they should have two envelopes with a thousand dollars in each one," Jake said to the remaining officer.

"Do you have such envelopes or do we need to search you?"

Capri and Ben looked at each other and pulled the envelopes out of their pockets.

"Here are the ones they gave me that supposedly have the money, but if you open them you can see it is just paper. The ones they have were pricked with my knife. One has one prick and the other has two pricks."

The female officer opened the envelopes that Jake had handed her and there were just strips of paper cut to the size of paper money.
She then opened the other two envelopes and there was money in both of them.

"He has tricked us," Capri said to the officer.

"Don't think so. We have heard it all and it is recorded. Jake has been on to you from the start. We followed you from the shopping center to this bank and have observed the whole thing. Not sure the lawyer will be able to get you out of this."

The other officer returned and said, "There are warrants out for your arrest in Virginia for scamming several people up there. We might not even get to try you here in North Carolina, but at least we will get you off the streets thanks to Jake's help. Please turn around and put your hands behind your back."

As the officers cuffed the two men they were read their rights and put into the police car.

"Jake, can you come down to the station and give us a statement even though we have most of it on tape? Also we will need to get you to sign some waivers so we can give you your money back."

"Sure, I think there is a third person involved, but I am not sure."

"Yeah, we have the license plate number and we will have another car pick her up. She has been observing from a distance after she dropped Ben off at the shopping center. They were pretty slick, but Jake you were slicker."

"Well you have to be aware if someone tries to make your greed work against you. When they promise you something for nothing you had better watch out. Normally people do not go around handing out $100 bills. It has been an interesting afternoon. I'll meet you at the station."

Jake followed the two officers to the station and went in with them. The officers introduced Jake to the chief, who thanked him for his help and complimented him on his quick thinking.

"When we contacted Malcolm, he said to trust

your lead that you were a good officer."

"I am a nature photographer now, but I guess I'll never get the FBI out of my system."

"He also said to tell you that there is nothing on John Wesley Williams yet. He told me a little of the story about your wife and parents. He is going to send us some information on Mr. Williams so we can keep our eyes out for him."

"He did threaten to come get me, but it was probably just all talk."

"You be careful. You have something that he thinks belongs to him and he just might try to get it back. From what Malcolm says he is pretty well connected with the mob and might have some help. Don't take any unnecessary chances."

"I need to get back to Ocean Isle. Sandy, my dog, will be wondering what has happened to me."

"We have all the information from you that we need in case we need your testimony, and you have your money back."

Jake shook the chief's hand and turned to leave when he remembered the $100 that Capri had given him.

"Chief, here is a $100 bill that Capri gave me for helping them. Don't I need to turn that in?"

"You keep that for your troubles today. He is not going to need that where he is going," the chief said as he waved Jake off.

On his drive back to Ocean Isle, Jake called Barbara and related the story of his afternoon adventure to her. Her only comment was, "You are a magnet for bad money. It just follows you around."

"I thought it was a pretty good April fool's joke that I played on those fellows."

Jake did not mention to her that he knew she was coming because he wanted to let it be a surprise, if she wanted it that way.

When Jake arrived at the cottage, Sandy met him at the door and let him know that he had been missed.

CHAPTER 8

A NIGHT WITH SUSAN

WEDNESDAY, APRIL 2, 2003 VERY EARLY A.M.

It was a warm night and the moon was very bright and Jake had been tossing and turning for a long time. He had a lot on his mind and was not able to get to sleep. On top of this, Sandy appeared at his bedside and indicated that she needed to go outside, which was very unusual for her.

When Jake opened the door and the gentle salt air breeze hit his face, he was completely awake.

"We might as well make the best of it and go for a walk on the beach as long as we are both up," Jake said to Sandy.

She looked up at him and wagged her tail as if to say, Yeah, that is what I had in mind.

Jake quickly dressed, put on some beach

shoes and in a minute they were making their way toward the ocean along the path through the dunes. The waves were pounding and the spray was flying in the moonlight as the waves crashed on the shore and rolled up the beach. The tide was coming in, but there was still a lot of beach left.

The pier, with one lone fisherman on it standing as a sentinel outlined against the bright clear sky was a beautiful picture that etched in Jake's mind. Looking back toward his house he caught some movement out of the corner of his eye. There, lumbering up the beach, was a huge loggerhead turtle making her way to lay her eggs. By instinct, Jake had picked up a small camera as he left the cottage. Being careful not to disturb the mother at work, Jake moved closer and began to take some pictures. A soft word to Sandy and she just stood by his side.

From what he had learned from Susan last year, he sensed that the mamma was going to stop short of having a safe place for her nest. The re-nourishment of the beach had caused changes and the steeper beach was more of a challenge for the loggerhead. She had stopped before getting to the high water line.

Jake glanced at his watch and it was about 3 a.m. What should he do? If she left her eggs there the tide would destroy the nest and all her work and the turtle eggs would be destroyed. Without hesitating, he started running toward his cottage calling Sandy to follow.

Inside, he went to the dresser and picked up his cell phone. He remembered he still had Susan's number on his speed dial from last summer. He was not sure what kind of response he would get, but was going to give it a try. Would she remember him? He sure had not forgotten her.

"Susan, please do not hang up, this is Jake Johnson. Do you remember me?"

"Yes, why are you calling at this hour?"

"Are you still interested in saving turtles?"

"Yes, but not so much at three in the morning. What's up?"

"Sandy, my dog, and I were talking a walk on the beach and found this big loggerhead laying her eggs well below the high tide line and we decided to call you to find out what to do. Sandy made me do it."

"Well good for Sandy. Where are you?"

"We are out in front of our cottage, Better Than Nutting."

"Do you have a shovel? All of my gear is at the museum and it would take a lot of time to get it and I do not want the tide to beat me to the eggs."

"I have a large one as well as a bunch of sand toys that renters have left at my place, including a lot of shovels and buckets."

"Get the big shovel, a rake and a couple of buckets and I'll meet you on the beach in a few minutes."

On his way out of the door he picked up a better camera, collected the shovel and rake and buckets from his utility room, and headed for the beach with Sandy close at his heels.

Mrs. Loggerhead was still there digging out her nest. Jake put the tools down and began taking pictures. She paid him no mind and went about her business as turtles have done for millions of years.

It was not long before he heard a car door slam and he started walking back to meet Susan.

He watched her appear over the sand dune. As she got closer he couldn't believe his eyes. At 3 a.m. she appeared to have stepped out of a fashion magazine.

Her blond hair was glistening in the moonlight. She was wearing a light blue button front tank top and a pair of London Jean fringed shorts set above the waist. She was barefooted. She was beautiful and Jake almost forgot why she was there.

"Hello Jake, Good to see you," Susan said as she stopped and gave him a big hug.

"Let's see what the lady is up to. We will have time to chat later."

By this time the turtle had finished laying the eggs and was laboriously covering them up.

"You were right to call me, Jake. In an hour or so the tide would have covered the nest and her tracks on the beach and we would have never known she was here."

Jake began to take pictures and he was taking as many of Susan as he was of the turtle who was now moving toward the ocean in her slow lumbering way. The huge turtle was awkward on land, but as soon as she hit the water she was a graceful creature in her own element.

Jake made an offer to help Susan, but knew from his last experience with her that she would do it all herself as she had been trained to do. He couldn't take his eyes off her and began to take pictures of her digging, bending, stretching and stopping as she dug the new hole and arranged the eggs in it just as they had been in the original nest.

"Jake, would you take this ribbon out of my pocket and tie my hair back in a pony tail? It is really bothering me, but my hands are so sandy I do not want to get the sand in my hair."

"Sure," Jake said as he took the ribbon hanging out of her pocket and tied her hair back out of her way. He caught a whiff of that same perfume she had been wearing last year when he had ridden behind her on the ATV as they searched the beach for turtles.

"That is much better," she said as she brushed some sand off her cheek with the back of her hand and gave Jake a thank you smile.

Jake laughed out loud as Susan jumped and screamed when Sandy nudged her leg with her wet nose. Once she realized what had happened, she laughed too and stopped to pet Sandy.

She continued to work and Jake continued to take pictures of her every move until she finally stood over the spot and said, "Well, that should do it until I can get back with some hardware cloth and stakes to secure the nest."

As they walked back to the cottage Jake said, "Why don't you stay and eat some breakfast with me and we can watch the sunrise? That is the least I can do for getting you out of bed so early."

"I am a mess, I'll just mess up your place with all the sand I have on me."

"You can take a shower while I cook us some pancakes and sausage. I can find something that you can slip into."

"Well, I am hungry and I don't have to go to work today. That sounds great."

Jake returned in a minute with some clothes, a towel and a bath cloth, but Susan was already in the outdoor shower.

"I'll hang these on the door and go make us some breakfast."

"Great, this shower feels wonderful. I'll be up in a minute."

As Jake finished setting the table on the porch, Susan came up the stairs with her hair wrapped up in the towel.

"Jake, do you have a comb I can use? I had more sand in my hair than I realized."

"Be right back," and in a moment Jake returned and handed her the comb.

"Like what you have done with the place."

"It's pretty simple, but Sandy and I have been enjoying being here."

"Can I help you do anything?"

"No, just have a seat and I'll be out in just a moment."

Just as the sun peeped up over the horizon, Jake returned with a tray of steaming pancakes, sausage, coffee and orange juice.

Sandy took her place between them on the floor, waiting for one of them to be sloppy and drop something.

"Jake, these pancakes are so light they almost float off the plate. What is your secret?"

"It is just a Betty Crocker recipe, but fresh ingredients including buttermilk do the trick. Glad you like them."

"Had heard you were on the island and was hoping you would call, but did not expect a 3 a.m. one"

"Sorry about that, but glad you did not hang up on me. I got involved with the chief and his homicide case as soon as I got back on the island and have been pretty busy."

"Has anything new happened? Through the gossip on the island I knew you were involved."

"No, we are still trying to find out if the fellows who left the body here also stayed on the island. We think they had taken him to a house somewhere on the island. We have checked out all the places that were rented through any of the agencies, but that still leaves a lot of homes that we do not know about."

As they sipped their coffee and watched the sun come up and paint the sky with all the beautiful colors, they were both silent for a few minutes.

"That was worth getting up for plus the satisfaction of having helped save a few more turtles," Susan said, smiling at Jake.

She began asking him questions about what

all that had happened to him since their meeting last year. She was filling in the blanks from what she had heard through the scuttlebutt on the beach.

He told her about finding his mom and dad after thinking they were dead and about the trials and the capturing of John Wesley Williams and of his escape. He did not bring up Barbara because he did not want to complicate his relationship with Susan. She might just remain a good friend, but he wanted to leave his options open.

Every now and then Sandy would stand up and nuzzle one of them for some attention and they would pet her and rub her head and she would lie back down knowing that she was not forgotten.

They chatted on and on like they had been friends for years and years until Susan finally looked at her watch and said to Jake, "I had better go. I do need to get some things done today. We will have to get together for another Frogmore Stew."

"I would really love that. I have had a good time telling people about that and no one had heard of it before."

"Jake, before I forget it, I have been thinking about you looking for the place where the killers might have been staying. I have seen lights on at a friend's place, but they are away on a cruise and they do not usually rent their place. It might bear checking into. The address is 273 West First Street."

Jake jotted the address down and said, "I'll look into that and let the chief know."

Susan gave Jake a big hug, a kiss on the cheek, squeezed his hand and said, " I have really enjoyed this and thank you for the call. Keep in touch."

Sandy demanded one last pet and Susan was out the door. Jake watched her get into her sports car and drive away, thinking again what a beautiful woman she was and wondering what would happen when she and Barbara met, which looked like it might happen sooner rather than later.

CHAPTER 9

THE VACANT BEACH HOUSE

APRIL 2, 2003 A.M.

"Come on, Sandy. Let's go check out the house Susan told us about."

Jake went to the nightstand and removed his pistol and tucked it into his belt in the small of his back and picked up a flashlight and placed it in his coat pocket.

As he drove to the address that Susan had given him, he noticed other cottages that might be prime locations for someone to break into without anyone seeing them.

He drove slowly past 273 West First Street, but couldn't see anything that might lead him to believe that anyone was still there. He parked his car a few houses down and put Sandy on a leash and began walking back to the house. He let Sandy stop and sniff and make her mark as he observed the surroundings. To anyone watching he would just be someone taking his dog out for a walk.

There was no activity anywhere around the house. No cars or construction crews working. He stopped on the sidewalk and noticed what appeared to be somewhat fresh tire tracks in the sandy area between the sidewalk and the pavement underneath the cottage. He avoided walking on them and went to the ocean side of the cottage and up the back stairs.

As he reached the top of the stairs he could see that the front door appeared to have been kicked in. He dropped Sandy's leash and reached for his gun. Moving slowly up the stairs and across the deck, he slowly pushed the broken door open and looked inside.

"Anyone home?" he yelled in a loud voice and then waited to see if he could hear any movement or noise at all. Nothing.

It was a typical old beach house with the living room and kitchen in the middle of the house, all open, and bedrooms and baths on each side. There was no one in the kitchen or living room area, but the furniture was out of place with a chair sitting in the middle of the room. He moved to his left and entered a bedroom where it looked like someone might have lain down on the bedspread. He went through the bathroom and into the other bedroom where he found pillows stacked up like someone might have read in the bed.

He crossed the kitchen, which was strewn

with drink and beer bottles and dirty dishes, and went into the other bedroom. He walked carefully through the bath and into the last bedroom and back into the living room.

He looked at the straight back chair with arms that was sitting in the middle of the room. There were remnants of duct tape on the chair and a pool of blood underneath the chair. A pillow with a dark brown hole in it was lying on the other side of the chair.

It certainly looked like this could be the place where Sergeant Farmer was held before he was shot and then dragged to the beach where he was found.

Sandy had followed Jake into the house and before she could disturb anything he took her back to the porch and tied her leash to the porch railing. Petting her on the head, he told her to stay and reached for his cell phone.

"Dan, this is Jake, put me through to the chief."

"Sure just a minute."

"Hello Jake, what's up?"

"Come to 273 West First Street. I think I have found where the murderers might have stayed on the island."

"I'll be right there."

Jake untied Sandy and took her downstairs and back to his truck and put her inside. He walked back to the cottage and stood on the sidewalk so that he could keep the chief from messing up the tire tracks under the house.

He was a little surprised that he did not hear any sirens as the chief drove up, but he decided that the chief was not as excitable as his deputy.

"How did you happen to find this?" the chief asked as he got out of the squad car.

"Susan, from the museum, told me she had seen cars and lights here and she knew that the owners were on a cruise. Sandy and I decided to check it out before we bothered you. It looks like there was something going on here even if it was not our fellows.

"Where is Sandy?"

"I put her back in the truck before she had an opportunity to mess up any evidence. She will be fine."

As they entered the house, Jake pointed out the broken door and the chief said, "The Mercers would never leave their place looking like this."

"Chief, we need to get the lab boys to come check this place out. This is still your investigation. Who should you get to come? The SBI, FBI or the NCSI? I am sure the FBI will want their fellows in on it, but it will take them longer to get here than the SBI or NCSI."

"Normally, I would call the SBI and I think that is what I'll do. We will let the others fight over it later."

Picking up his radio, he called Dan and said, "Dan, Call the SBI and tell them we need a lab crew at Ocean Isle Beach as soon as possible. Jake has found the house where the killers might have stayed. When you have finished making that call, come down here and tape off the crime scene area."

"Be right there, Chief."

As an after thought the chief said, "No sirens, and please be careful. We do not need another busted squad car."

The chief smiled at Jake and said, "I am never going to let him live that down."

Jake chuckled out loud.

"I am going down to keep Dan from messing up the tire tracks and to get some pictures of them before they get messed up. I think he has replenished the supplies in the casting kit and I'll have him get some impressions of the tire tracks."

As the chief went downstairs, Jake called John and said, "John, we have found the house where they must have kept Sergeant Farmer. It looks like he was shot here. Tell Malcolm. He might want to get the lab boys down here. The chief has already contacted the SBI and they will be sending a crew."

"We are getting ready to leave and will see you this afternoon. Have you gotten the 'frogs' yet?" John laughingly said to Jake.

"Not yet, but I'll not let you starve."

As Jake finished the call, Dan came upstairs with his camera in his hand.

"Hello Jake. Looks like you stumbled on the mother load"

"Yeah, it sure looks like either this is the place

or we have another crime that has been committed."

"The chief has gone back to the office. He said to tell you he would talk to you later. He wants me to stay here until we can secure the place. As soon as I get these pictures I'll make the cast of the tire tracks. Also found some footprints in the blown-in sand where they got out of the car."

"That's good. Can I help you with anything? Looks like there will be plenty of DNA to help find these people. I would suggest that you leave the fingerprinting to the experts. They have more sophisticated equipment. I don't think we should leave this house unmanned until the lab boys get here. We do not want some curious person wandering in and contaminating the crime scene before we get all the information we can. I am going back to the cottage, but if you need any relief give me a call and I can come back and stay for a while."

"Thanks Jake, if I need you I'll call."

Sandy was resting with her head out the window when Jake went back to his truck, but as soon as she saw him she was up wagging her tail in excitement.

"Did you think I had forgotten you?" Jake said as he petted her and slipped into the seat beside her.

Before going back to his cottage, Jake made a quick trip into Shallotte to Belk's to pick up another set of sheets. In all the excitement of the day before, he had forgotten to get the bed sheets he needed. He picked out some bright red ones that felt silky and thought they would be something Barbara would like. He had everything else he needed and in a few minutes he was back at his place.

CHAPTER 10

THE FBI's IN TOWN

APRIL 3, 2003

In the late afternoon, Sandy perked up her ears and went to the door. Jake heard a car door slam and got out of his chair and went to the window. John and Barbara were getting their bags out of the car. Jake opened the door and Sandy bolted out, heading straight for Barbara. She dropped her bags, gave Sandy a big hug, rubbed her head, and shook her paw. They both were glad to see each other.

"Well, I know who has been missed," John said to Barbara.

"The feeling is mutual," Barbara said to John, but her face lit up in a big smile as Jake came down the stairs.

"Hello there. Glad you are here," Jake said to both of them as he went over and hugged Barbara and she kissed him on the cheek.

John put down his bags and shook Jake's hand and then they both hugged. There had been mutual respect and friendship for a long time.

Jake picked up Barbara's bags and they all headed up the stairs.

"So this is 'Better than Nutting,'" she said as she read the sign at the back door.

"Sandy and I really love it here. We are not finished fixing it up, but we have all the comforts of home plus a beautiful view of the ever-changing ocean. John, your room is to the right and Barbara, we will let you have the other half of the cottage on the left."

"This is great," Barbara and John said almost in unison.

"I got excited about your coming and I went ahead and made your beds. The towels and everything you will need are in the bathroom. If you need anything please let me know. It has been a while since Sandy and I have had house guests."

" We are not guests and you do not have to wait on us." Barbara said quickly.

"Speak for yourself, Barbara," John said, "I am going to let him wait on me."

"When are the lab boys coming?" Jake asked, to change the subject.

"They will be here first thing in the morning. They will be coming out of Myrtle Beach."

"They will have a lot of stuff to process, but the crime scene is small and it shouldn't take them too long. Hope we can get identification out of all the mess they left. I want to get this wrapped up. I am anxious to get back to the mountains."

"You just want to be ready for John Wesley when he shows up," John said with a big smile on his face.

"He is no laughing matter. He is a dangerous man'" Barbara said with a frown on her face.

"Without you there to protect me I do feel a little vulnerable. I might have to get Jimbo back if you are not going to be there."

"Do you hear that John, I am being replaced by a dog."

"Wait, I don't like the way this conversation is going. Why don't you settle in and then we will go get some supper."

"You haven't found enough frogs yet to feed us," John said as he perpetuated the joke about the Frogmore stew.

"Thought we would go to Calabash tonight for some real seafood. I'll fix something here at the house later."

Jake fed Sandy and hollered, "I m going to take Sandy for a walk. I'll be right back."

As Jake and Sandy walked down the sidewalk, a car came to a stop and Susan said, "Hello Jake. See you have company."

"Yeah, the FBI team is here and they are staying with me. It is good to see John, my old partner."

He purposefully did not mention Barbara, but realized that Susan would hear about her in the very near future.

"Got to run. Enjoyed the other morning and appreciated the good breakfast," Susan said smiling as she slowly drove away.

"O.K. Sandy. Let's go feed these hungry folks."

As Jake walked in, Barbara asked, " Who was that good looking gal in the sports car? A friend of Sandy's?"

"She is the head of the museum, I met her when I was taking pictures of the turtles," Jake said, trying to be nonchalant about it, but he caught the twinkle in Barbara's eye and knew she was playing him.

John said, "I see you made us some fried apple pies. I had to try one."

"That was going to be your dessert when we got back from Captain Nance's?"

"What are fried apple pies?" Barbara asked.

"I'll tell you about them later. We need to go before it gets dark. There are some things I would like to show you."

Jake took them by the house at 273 West First Street, but did not stop. The patrol car was there and the area was all covered in yellow tape. As they passed the motel, Jake pointed out where the body was found and showed them the police station over by city hall.

Driving over the bridge, Barbara and John

were awestruck by the beauty of the waterway and the surrounding marshes. The sky was getting ready for a beautiful sunset and one lone boat was leaving its wake behind as it was making its way down the waterway.

They went left at the light and took a detour down to Gause Landing where Jake showed them the log cabin that was for sale that he had thought about buying. Barbara and John couldn't get over the beautiful drive down the dirt road underneath the large oaks with Spanish moss hanging almost to the top of the truck. It looked like a picture from 'Gone With the Wind'. Barbara had never seen anything like that before except in pictures. The old historic homes on the road also caught her eye.

"This is a place I would love to paint." Barbara said wistfully.

"No reason you can't," Jake said, hoping she would come stay with him a while.

"Are you going to invest some of John Wesley Williams money in that cabin?" John asked jokingly.

"Well I reckon I had better do something with it before he comes and tries to take it back, since you folks can't seem to keep him in custody," Jake answered back.

Back on the main road, Jake pointed out the grocery store, the Planetarium, Bill's Fresh Seafood Market, and the Sunset Beach drawbridge which would be gone in a few weeks.

"This is the last drawbridge on the waterway. Most of the people who own houses on the island did not want a bridge, but the authorities keep pushing for one, citing safety reasons. The bridge opens on the hour for regular boat traffic and as necessary for commercial traffic. My grandfather who used to live just down the road had a hard time sleeping so he would come over about 4 a.m. and play gin rummy with the bridge tender."

"So you grew up coming down here?" Barbara asked.

"Yes. They sold out and moved back to the piedmont, but I have a lot of great memories of these beaches."

John spoke up, "There are golf courses everywhere. They are so beautiful it makes one want to play golf just to be able to walk around on them."

"A lot of people from up north come down in the winter to play golf here and at Myrtle Beach."

"You are not going to tell us another of your bad jokes about the Yankees, are you?" Barbara asked.

"Did I touch a nerve? Well then here is one on the lighter side.
Mr. Winberg came home unexpectedly and found his wife in bed with another man. Furious, he cried, 'What are you doing?' 'See,' said Mrs. Winberg turning to her lover, 'I told you he was stupid.'"

"OK. OK. Enough of your jokes," Barbara said smiling at Jake and winking at John.

"All right. There is another place I want you to see, but we are a little late to get the full picture tonight. There is a pond back behind these golf courses on your right where the egrets come to nest every night. It is a beautiful sight to see all those big white birds flying in and covering all the trees in the area. Barbara, it would also make a beautiful place to paint."

As they entered Calabash, John exclaimed, "Look at all these seafood restaurants. How in the world do they all make a profit?"

"In the peak season you probably would have to stand in line at most of them," Jake answered.

"Do they all use local seafood?" Barbara asked.

"Probably in season yes, but the local joke is that the same wholesale truck delivers frozen seafood to all the restaurants, but the patrons swear that their favorite restaurant has better seafood than the others. You go figure."

"Do you have a favorite?" John asked.

"Have eaten at most of them, but probably go to Captain Nance's most often. It has a good view and will serve anyone the Senior Citizen platters."

John smiled and said, "Hope it is not like the restaurant I was at last week when the waiter brought my steak and was holding it down with his thumb. 'Are you crazy?' I yelled at him, 'you have your thumb on my steak.' The waiter yelled back at me, 'Do you want it to fall on the floor again?'"

Barbara and Jake burst out laughing and Barbara said," Enough is enough, let's go eat, I am starving."

The waitress seated them at a table overlooking the water where the boats were tied up and a few people were milling around on the dock.

"You have any suggestions?" Barbara asked.

"Well, of course, I like it all because I grew up eating it. Their portions are large so I always order the Senior Citizen's platter which is still a lot of food and they do have a variety of things that you can get."

"Since it is March. I was expecting to see a lot of steamed oysters," John said.

"You are right, the 'R' months are the right time, but would suggest we go to an oyster bar if that is what you want. We can do that another time."

After they had made their choices and placed their orders, they grazed on the hot fresh hush puppies and drank the syrupy sweet iced tea until their food came and then the three were lost in the enjoyment of a great southern seafood meal.

As they finished their meal they reminisced about old times for a while and then decided it was time to get back to the cottage.

Sandy was waiting for them at the door and after getting attention from everyone, she made her exit down the stairs.

"Jake, I saw your Woodrow over on the table, are you up for some picking and signing? Barbara asked.

"Only if John will sing with us," Jake answered.

"What about our fried apple pies? I can't sing on an empty stomach," John quipped.

The two laughed and rolled their eyes at John and then Barbara said, "You were going to tell me about the fried apple pies."

"My grandmother taught me to make them a long time ago. Pretty simple. I make the dough from flour, baking powder and milk. I just add a little milk at a time until I get the mixture into a soft dough. I put that in the fridge while I prepare the apples. I take a couple of cups of Pink Lady dried apples and add sugar, cinnamon, nutmeg, a pinch of salt and a little water and let them cook until they are soft and dry. Then you take the dough and divide it out into ten or so balls and roll them out with a rolling pin into little circles. Add the apples and fold over and secure the edges so it looks like a little half moon. Take an iron frying pan and add Crisco and when it gets hot you cook the pies until they are golden brown on both sides. Put them out on some paper towels and then begin eating them with some ice-cold milk. Some people like to eat a little cheese with them. Later you can eat them cold or heat them up a little. Are you ready to try them or would you rather pass?"

"The only passing I am going to do is pass the plate after I get mine," John said as he retrieved the milk from the fridge.

"What's your pleasure, Barbara? Do you want it cold or hot?"

"I'll just try it cold. I have always enjoyed cold apple pie and this sounds like the same thing."

The ooh's and ah's came as John and Barbara bit into the freshly made pies.

77

"If you keep on, Jake, you will make a good wife for someone," John said, smiling.

The three sang a little, talked a lot and stayed away from business until late in the evening. Barbara and Jake took Sandy for a walk and had a few quiet moments to themselves.

CHAPTER 11

CHECKING OUT THE CRIME SCENE

APRIL 4, 2003

When Barbara returned form her morning run on the beach Jake was busy making breakfast and John was just getting out of the shower.

"What is that in front of your place with the iron stakes and the yellow ribbon?" Barbara asked. It looks like a crime scene."

"That is the turtle nest that we fixed the other night. In about three months there will be a lot of little turtles boiling out of it. Quite a sight. Sandy and I saw the mother laying her eggs and called the turtle people and they came and relocated the nest so the high tide wouldn't destroy it."

Jake hedged on the whole truth because he was not ready to try to explain about Susan just yet.

To change the subject Jake asked, "Are you

ready for breakfast or do you want to take your shower first?"

"If John is ready we can eat now and I can shower later."

"I'll start the pancakes then." Jake said.

As they ate their breakfast they began to talk about the case and why they were there. Jake brought them up to date on what he knew about the case. The personalities involved, and the interesting interplay between the different agencies.

As they were clearing off the table, Jake got a phone call from Ken, the Buncolm County Sheriff, and Barbara and John listened to the one- sided conversation.

"Well, hello Ken, how are you?

"Guess who is here, Barbara and John."

"I'll tell them you said hello," Jake said, smiling at John and Barbara.

"When did that happen?"

"Have any idea of who it might have been?

"Did they actually go in?

"Well that's good."

"I plan to be back up there in a few days."

"No, they do not have any leads on John Wesley Williams."

"Have you any reason to think it might have been him?"

"Well there is nothing in the cabin of any real value."

"Thanks for keeping me informed and I'll call as soon as I get back. It is getting time to do some fly-fishing. Give your sweet wife a hug for me," Jake said as he hung up the phone.

"Well, as you know, that was Ken. Someone has been messing around my cabin, but did not go inside and did not really do any damage at all. He has no idea who it might have been. There was nothing to link it to John Wesley. He is going to increase the patrols until I get back. Ken is a good friend. I appreciate his interest in helping me."

"It is a pretty good chance that John Wesley Williams has paid you an initial call. You need to be extra careful when you do get back. Do you think he knows about this place at the beach?" Barbara asked.

"I doubt it. No one around Blackberry Inn knows about it."

"I am going to call Malcolm and let him know about your visitor because it might be a lead on where your friend is holding out," John said.

"We need to get on over to the chief's office and check in with him before the lab boys arrive," Barbara said, getting back to the business at hand.

In a few minutes the showers were taken, Sandy had her walk, and they were all ready to go.

At the Police Station, Jake introduced John and Barbara to Dan and then took them back to the chief's office and made introductions again.

Jake looked around to see if Ms. Townsend was around, but did not see her anywhere.

John informed the chief about the lab boys and said they should be arriving shortly. The chief told him that the SBI had already been and made their investigation, but had left the scene intact for the feds.

As they finished up, Dan came in with the two fellows from the Myrtle Beach office and made introductions all around. Doug Lucas and Jim Boone had been with the agency a long time and had kind of retired to the Myrtle Beach area where the call for their services was not as great as it had been when they worked together in LA. Neither John and Barbara nor Jake had ever met them before.

"Escort this crew down to the house and help them with anything they need," the chief said to Dan.

Dan led the three-car procession down to the house and they all congregate inside after taking some pictures of the tire tracks underneath the cottage.

Even though the SBI fellows out of Raleigh had already been there, the scene looked the same as Jake remembered it except for the remains of some white powder that they had dusted around looking for fingerprints.

"Did the SBI come up with anything special?" Jake asked Dan.

"No. They were still looking for something to help identify the two people when I last talked to them. Even though these thugs were messy, they must have picked up the shell casing. The SBI did get enough DNA to make a match with the victims clothes so we know that he was tied to that chair and it was his blood on the floor."

As Jake and Dan were talking, Jake heard Barbara call to Jim to come over because she had found a shell casing. Barbara lifted up a rocking chair, and buried in the carped underneath the rocker was a casing. Jim took his tweezers and picked it up and put it into an evidence bag.

"Well, Miss Sharp Eyes found what the experts had not been able to locate," Jake said, teasing Barbara. "Good job."

"That will help establish that he was killed here and taken to the beach. The DNA should help place the two goons in both places. Now all we need to know is who they are," John said to the group.

"Just found a good fingerprint that I have sent to the bureau to see if they can get a match," Bill said.

Dan got a call on his radio, "Yes, Chief. You say his name is Sam McLean. Well, we have some good news also. Barbara found a shell casing and they have found a print in the room that matches a partial print on the shell casing. Things are looking up. We will come back to the station as soon as they finish."

"The SBI has identified one of the fellows as Sam McLean who is wanted in South Carolina for armed robbery. The chief wants everyone to stop back by the office before they leave the island."

"Has anyone notified JAG about these findings?" John asked.

"Not sure what the chief has done," Dan

replied.

Doug and Jim continued their investigation, taking pictures and collecting samples from various things and in a few minutes they indicated they had done all they could. Dan secured the building and the group headed back to the police station. The chief assembled them in his conference room and asked what they had found.

"We got prints that confirm that Sam McLean definitely was at the scene and we also got prints that show that Jimmy Spivey was there. The victim's prints were on the arms of the chair he was tied to and it was his blood on the floor. The partial print from the casing Barbara found has been sent to the lab and they are trying to match it to either Jimmy or Sam. There were several other prints that do not show up in any of the databases. Probably from the owners or renters of the cottage. We have concluded that they stayed in the cottage about three days, but left on the day Sergeant Farmer was killed. They were a messy group and probably did not think about this place being linked to the shooting. We are waiting on the lab to definitely say that the shell casing came from the murder weapon. One of these fellows loaded the gun even if he did not pull the trigger. The lab verified that the gun had been wiped clean and Sergeant Farmers prints were the only ones on the gun, but there is no way he could have shot himself. With the fingers broken the way they were, there is not a way he could have held the gun. We think that the lab will be able to match a pair of vice grip pliers to the breaking of the fingers. The pliers had both Jimmy and Sam's prints on them. They were in the back of a kitchen drawer and had not been noticed by the SBI. The lab is still trying to determine the kind of car from the tracks underneath the building. That is what we found in a nut shell," Jim told the group.

"Where do we go from here? We now know who the two crooks are, but how do we find them?" the chief asked.

"The JAG team might be helpful. They are investigating the possible thefts and these fellows must have been in South Carolina to have been aware of Sergeant Farmer and his movements," Jake indicated to the group.

"The FBI has put out an all points bulletin for these two," John said.

"The body has been released to JAG and we can clear up the crime scene and give the house back to its owners," the chief said.

Officer Townsend came to the door and motioned for the chief, who excused himself and left the room. He returned in a few minutes and reported to the group.

"JAG has the last known addresses of the two suspects and are working with the local authorities in South Carolina to try to locate them. They think it will be just a matter of time. There is no indication that the two realize they have been identified with the murder. JAG has not determined whether there were other people involved."

"They were pretty sloppy and I think they were

probably just the thugs who were hired by someone to get information from Sergeant Farmer and they got carried away and killed him. We don't know if they got any information or not. I definitely think we should also be looking for the person or persons who hired them," Barbara said to the group.

"Well, we thank you fellows and lady for your help and I think we are done here for today. I'll keep you informed if anything else comes up and I expect the same from you," the chief said, pushing his chair back from the table and getting up.

The rest of the group gathered their notes and after saying their goodbyes the group dispersed.

John stopped to use the phone to call Malcolm and let him know what was happening while Jake and Barbara went outside.

"This is getting solved way too fast. We are not going to have much time together," Jake said to Barbara.

"Looks like we are going to have to make some time if we want to see each other," Barbara replied as John came out the door.

"Malcolm wants us to go up to Columbia in the morning and touch base with the JAG team to see if we can help find those two criminals. Here are a couple of photos that had just come in on the wire of our two suspects. Here are copies for you too Jake."

Barbara read the description out loud. "Jimmy Spivey, birthplace Hoke County, North Carolina 1967, white male, 35, 230 pounds, 5 feet 9 inches, brown hair, hazel eyes, scar on his left cheek, tattoo of a snake on the back of his right hand. Graduated Hoke County High School 1985, last know address 334 Kimberly Street, Columbia, South Carolina. Apartment now vacant. Divorced 5 years, no children, wife living in Fayetteville, North Carolina. Former military stationed at Fort Jackson, last duty, clerk in paymaster's office, discharged 1989. Last employer White Trucking Lines left June 2000, suspect in armed robbery in 2001, no convictions. "

John began to read, "Sam McLean, birthplace Hoke County North Carolina 1966, Graduated Hoke County High School 1984, white male, 36, 209 pounds, 6 feet 1 inch, sandy hair, blue eyes, no distinguishing marks. Last known address 2346 Hay Street, Fayetteville North Carolina. Apartment vacant. Former military stationed at Fort Bragg, North Carolina, clerk in paymaster's office discharged 1989. Last employer Sanford Brick, truck driver discharged July 2000."

"Looks like these two fellows knew each other and had worked in the paymaster's office at two different bases and probably concocted this plan to get rich stealing from the Army," Jake said to Barbara and John.

"They have a presence in the two communities so they probably will not be to hard to find. Doesn't sound like they will be trying to leave the country or anything. Probably don't realize that we would be on to them so quickly," Barbara added.

The three left the station and returned to Jake's cottage where Sandy was patiently waiting for them and enjoyed the attention she got from all three, but she especially played up to Barbara who had always given her a lot of attention.

"Since you two will be leaving in the morning, we better have our Frogmore Stew tonight. I am going to Bill's Seafood Market to get some shrimp. Anyone care to go?" Jake asked John and Barbara.

"If is all right, I think I'll take a little walk on the beach. Is it all right if I take Sandy?" John asked.

"Sure, she will love that, but you better put her on a leash," Jake answered.

"I'll ride with you," Barbara said.

On the ride to the store Jake and Barbara made tentative plans to see each other back in Weaverville in a couple of weeks. These long distance relationships can leave a lot to be desired, but they were both willing to try it for a while and see what would happen.

All the fresh seafood she saw in the showcases at Bill's intrigued Barbara. Jake explained the finer points of the different fish, but Barbara was more fascinated by all the crabs. Coming from the North, she was not used to seeing such a variety of seafood outside of the Red Lobster Restaurant even though in Washington she had a chance to try different things from Chesapeake Bay.

Before returning to the cottage, Jake took Barbara over the drawbridge to Sunset Beach. The new bridge would be open soon and there would be no more drawbridge. He told her how the beach was changing and building up, while a lot of beaches were washing away. He showed her where the old Civil War wreck was before it got covered up with sand. He pointed out the house his parents used to own and reminisced about the good times he had had as a youngster swimming and fishing and just enjoying the beach.

Back at the cottage, Barbara opted for a run on the beach and Jake began to prepare supper. John and Sandy had not returned from their walk.

"If you see John, tell him supper will be ready in about an hour."

Jake assembled the corn, sausage, and potatoes and got everything ready for the pot. He decided to make a little slaw and grated the cabbage, added Miracle Whip, salt and a little vinegar and it was good to go. He put his big pot on the stove and added the potatoes and sausage and then set the table by spreading out newspapers and placing the plates and silverware on top. He was sure Barbara and John were going to wonder about all this. He normally would peel the shrimp, but decided to let everyone get the full effect by letting them peel their own. He placed John and Barbara where they could see out the window and would be able to enjoy the beautiful scene of the ever-changing ocean.

Jake poured himself a glass of tea and sat on the porch while he awaited their return. He watched the pelicans dive for food and the sand pipers run up and down the beach playing tag with the waves. He was lost in his thoughts when he heard Barbara come up the stairs.

"You going to shower before supper?" Jake asked as she washed off her feet in the tub by the porch railing.

"Believe I will if I have time."

"Sure. We have no timetable. Is John coming?"

"Yeah, with no one else on the beach he has been having fun throwing things in the water for Sandy to retrieve."

"If he waits for her to get tired, he will be out there a long time."

"How was your run?"

"I turned up the speed and made it to the point and back. I am learning to love the beach."

"That's great. It is a relaxing place."

John and Sandy came trudging up the walk and it looked like Sandy still had more energy than John.

"I ended up letting her go into water, do I need to give her a bath?"

"I'll take care of that, you just get ready for supper. Barbara is taking a shower. Try the downstairs shower. It is wonderful with the nice breeze blowing while the warm water covers you."

When they had assembled again with everyone feeling fresh and clean, Jake added the shrimp to the pot of corn, sausage, and potatoes.

"Ran out of placemats, did you, Jake?" John joked as he looked at the newspaper-covered table.

"No. It will just make the cleaning up process go a lot easier and I know what messy eaters you and Barbara are. How about poring the tea while I separate the vegetables into separate bowls?"

Jake had added cocktail sauce, melted butter and saltine crackers, and fried cornbread to the table.

"This looks like a feast. So this is the famous Frogmore Stew," Barbara said as they began to pass the food around

"Don't get him started about this stew. He will make up some wild tale that you won't believe," John said, laughing as he started to peel his shrimp.

As they all dug into the supper, enjoying the shrimp, corn, potatoes and sausage, Jake said to them, "Seeing you both enjoying your food so much reminds me of a good reducing exercise I recently heard about. It just consists of placing both hands against the table edge and pushing back."

"Jake, can't you let us eat in peace?" Barbara said, laughing.

"I am not going to push back until I get some more of that good cornbread." John said.

"How do you make this cornbread?" Barbara asked.

"It is real simple. You take some self-rising yellow corn meal and add a little salt and mix it with water until it is pretty thin. Set it aside for a few minutes and get some grease hot in an iron skillet. Pour in a small amount of the cornmeal mixture, making sure it spreads out in a thin layer, and when it is done on one side, flip it over. If it is thin enough there will be little holes formed around the outside edge. Then you take it out put it in a dish with paper towels to let it drain. It will drain better if you stand it on its side. Really simple to make and it goes so well with this meal. It also goes well with greens and collards."

After they had finished the stew and John had indulged himself in a couple of fried apple pies and the plates and silverware were removed from the table, Jake started to fold up the newspapers that contained the shrimp shells and the corn cobs, put it all into a plastic bag, and took it downstairs to the garbage can.

Back upstairs, John and Barbara flopped down on the couch and told Jake how much they had enjoyed their meal.

"That was fun," Jake said. "I love to see people enjoy their food and this is such an easy meal to prepare. I still haven't figured out why they called it frogmore stew."

"Well buddy, I am one up on you. I did a little research and found that back in the 60's, Richard Gay, owner of Gay Fish Company of St. Helena Island in South Carolina is credited with coming up with Frogmore Stew. As you know, it does not contain any frogs, but was named after the little town where Gay lived. . When the post office canceled service to Frogmore and just rolled it into Beaufort, some people started calling the dish Beaufort Stew or Low Country Boil, but the diehards will always call it Frogmore Stew. Now you have, 'the rest of the story.'"

"Well, thank you Mr. Hardin for enlightening us

on this subject."

"Since you people are leaving tomorrow to go up to Fort Jackson, I am going to take a little run up to Raleigh and Hillsville, Virginia. I promised my dad I would check on the house while they are on their cruise and I want to touch base with the Farmers and let them know what we have found out about the case. I'll probably spend the night and meet you back here in a couple of days if Malcolm does not drag you back to Washington."

"I know his parents will be relieved to know he did not commit suicide," Barbara said.

"It shouldn't be too long before we catch the two thugs," John added.

"I am going to take Sandy for a little walk. Anyone care to join me?" Jake asked.

"Not me. I am going to turn in," John said.

"I'll go," Barbara said as she slipped into her jacket.

By this time Sandy had figured out what was happening and was standing by the door ready to go. As they walked out on the deck and down the stairs, Jake took Barbara's hand and quietly said to her, "It is so nice to have you here. I have missed you."

She squeezed his hand and gave him a kiss on the cheek and said, "I have missed you too."

They ended up on the pier sitting on a fisherman's perch and watching the waves break on the shore, enjoying the solitude and gazing at the star-filled sky. Jake thought that there were still not many lights in the houses up and down the beach, but in a few months the place would be brimming with people. They enjoyed the time together until Sandy got restless and they headed back to the cottage.

CHAPTER 12

TRIP TO HILLSVILLE

FRIDAY APRIL 5, 2003

Jake and Sandy took the back roads through the country, stopping at Melvin's in Elizabethtown for a quick burger. Jake enjoyed the countryside and especially the lush dark green fields of rye and the colorful fields of red and purple sourgrass. The trip was uneventful and they arrived in Raleigh looking forward to a quick stop at Burke Bros Hardware. That was Jake's favorite store and he knew that he could always find what he wanted without all the hassle of going into one of the big box stores. The folks who worked there called most of their customers by their first name and even after several years absence, a couple of them recognized Jake when he entered the store. His father was a regular visitor and they had kept up with Jake through him. Sure enough, Jake found the special door closer he was looking for and picked up some screen wire to repair a screen at his cabin in Weaverville. Looking around he was still amazed at all the items they carried. The store had opened in 1936 and was now run by the families of the original owners. A bag of fresh popped corn and he was on his way.

His parent's house in Cary was all snug just like they left it. He watered some plants and checked all the windows and doors to be sure nothing was amiss. He fixed himself a frozen pot pie, fed Sandy, and sat down in his dad's recliner to catch the news. He was awakened by Sandy, who was nudging him and reminding him that she needed to go outside before he went down for the night.

He was up early and fed Sandy, but decided he would just pick up a Bojangles biscuit on his way out of town. The Research Triangle traffic was even worse than he remembered, but it was not long before he was passed it and into the flow of traffic on Highway 40. In Winston Salem he made the turn onto Highway 52 and it was not long before Pilot Mountain was visible on his left and the mountains where Hanging Rock State Park was appeared on his right. It was a beautiful drive and as he passed through Mount Airy. the Blue Ridge Mountains loomed ahead of him. Old Highway 52 made for a much more scenic route than the new Highway 77, allowing him to catch a glimpse of Stone Mountain off to the left every now and then. At the top of the mountain he resisted the urge to stop at a fruit stand and decided that would be his treat on the way home.

When he turned off onto highway 221 toward Hillsville, he decide it would be polite to call the Farmers and let them know he was almost there. It had been a long time since he had been in Hillsville. The last time had been when he was in college visiting an old friend, Jim Thompson. They had taken in the big flea market and done some fishing in Jim's dad's pond.

As he drove up the long drive to the Farmers' house, he appreciated the beautiful view they had looking out over the rolling countryside. When he stopped and opened the door, Sandy bounded out of the truck and met Mrs. Farmer coming out to meet them.   Sandy had endeared herself to them when they had met at the beach. Mrs. Farmer gave Jake a hug and told him that Mr. Farmer had gone to the store and would be right back.

Jake made small talk because he did not want to have to repeat himself when he told them about all that had happened since he last saw them at the beach.

In a few minutes, Mr. Farmer came in and gave Sandy a pat on the head and shook Jake's hand. They sat around the kitchen table and Mrs. Farmer plied him with fresh-made cookies and fresh milk from their cows.

Jake related what had happened and told them that the thugs had tried to get information about the army payroll from their son, but as far as they could tell at this time he had not given them any information. Jake gave them a copy of the death certificate and told them the body would be released to them any time they were ready.

Mr. Farmer indicated that he had already been in contact with the local funeral home and they were in the process of making the arrangements.

Mr. Farmer attempted to pay Jake for all his troubles, but Jake would have none of it. He assured them it was just a matter of time and they would have the responsible parties behind bars.

Mrs. Farmer said, "I know justice will be done, but nothing they do can bring Harry back to us."

"No, but at least now we can try to get some closure to this." Mr. Farmer replied

They both insisted that Jake stay longer, but he explained that he needed to get on the road because he had a long drive back to Ocean Isle. Mrs. Farmer packed him a snack and slipped Sandy a cookie as they went out the door.

The mountain fruit stand produced some eating apples as well as some dried Pink Lady apples for more fried apple pies. Jake settled in and it was not long before he was back in the drudgery of big highway driving. He waited until he got to Stephenson's Bar-B-Que outside Raleigh before he stopped again. It was Thursday and he knew that their special for today was chicken stew, green beans and candied yams and good sweet tea. Sandy resented having to stay in the truck, but did not stay mad long when he brought her some of the leftover hush puppies.

On Highway 95 outside of Fayetteville, Jake made a pit stop at the rest area. As he was washing his hands, a man beside him caught his eye. On the back of his hand was a snake tattoo, and there was a scar on his left cheek. This all clicked into place in his detective brain and he knew he was looking at Jimmy Spivey, one of the men they were looking for in the Ocean Isle Beach killing.

As the man started to leave, Jake shouted after him, "Jimmy Spivey. I haven't seen you since Hoke Mills High".

Jimmy stopped and turned around." Do I know you?"

"You might not remember me. I was an assistant coach and had you in gym class."

"I really don't recall you, but you seem to know who I am," Jimmy said as they walked out of the building toward the parking lot.

Jake was trying to stall to see if there was anyone else with him, and by the time they reached the cars Jake determined that he was alone. When Jimmy started to open his car door, Jake slammed it shut with his foot, reached in the back of his belt and got out his gun, and pushed Jimmy onto the car with his gun in his back.

Jimmy yelled out loud, ""What are you doing?"

"If you take your hands off the car, I'll make your birth certificate a worthless document" Jake said to him very sternly.

Jake checked to see that Jimmy did not have any weapons, and then retrieved his cell phone from his pocket and dialed 911.

"This is Jake Johnson. I am at the southbound rest stop on Highway 95 and have Jimmy Spivey, a murder suspect, in custody. Please send an officer immediately. We will be in a white Ford pickup.

"Are you crazy?" Jimmy yelled. "I don't know what you are talking about"

"Just be quiet and stand still."

Jimmy made a move like he might run for it and Jake said, "Can you run faster than 1200 feet per second? Because that's the speed of the bullet that will be chasing you."

Jimmy calmed down and Jake took him to his truck and told him to lie down in the truck bed. Sandy watched what was happening from the rear window.

"Where is your buddy Sam McLean?"

"I'm not talking to you," Jimmy said between a few choice cuss words.

In a few minutes Jake saw the trooper coming toward him with his lights flashing.

The trooper got out of the car with his gun drawn and asked Jake to put down his weapon. Jake put it on the ground. The officer reached down and picked it up and asked Jake to explain what was happening. Jake gave the trooper the whole story and suggested he call Chief Prevatte at Ocean

Isle Beach to verify his story or call Malcolm at the FBI Bureau in Washington DC.

The trooper got Jimmy out of the truck bed and asked for some identification. After looking at his driver's license, he told him to turn around and he put handcuffs on him and took him to the back seat of his car.

"We got the bulletin on him just yesterday. How did you find him?"

"I was just lucky. I saw him in the men's room and recognized him from his picture. I have been working with Chief Prevatte on the case. I am a former FBI agent and my two FBI friends are down at Camp Jackson trying to find this fellow and his buddy, Sam McLean, who killed an army Sergeant at Ocean Isle Beach."

"Here is your gun back. Lucky some tourist did not smack you in the head thinking you were robbing this guy. You handled it very well."

"Where will you take Jimmy?"

"They probably will have me take him to Fayetteville until they decide what to do with him. Let me get some information from you so I can write up my report."

Jake filled in the details for Officer Rodgers and they chatted for a minute and then the officer left for Fayetteville. Jake pushed Barbara's button on his cell phone and when she answered Jake said, " Guess what. I just found Jimmy Spivey at a rest stop on Highway 95 and the highway patrol officer is on his way to Fayetteville to deposit him in the jail. What about them apples?"

"You're kidding," Barbara said, dumbfounded.

"Y'll had any luck with Sam McLean?"

"Not yet. But with Jimmy in custody it should become easier depending on who pulled the trigger."

"Yeah, one of these bad boys will be wanting to make a deal. Are you two coming back to Ocean Isle tonight?"

"Probably not, with this development, we probably will go to Fayetteville to question Jimmy and see if we can get a lead on Sam."

"If I had known this would take you away, I probably would have just let him go."

"You nut. I'll see you again soon, I promise."

"Tell John I enjoyed our short visit. I love you."

Jake hung up before Barbara could answer. He was a little surprised he had said that because he was not sure he was ready for any kind of commitment yet. But it was done and he would live with the consequences because he did know that Barbara was beginning to fill a void in his life since he had lost Jackie.

Jake called Chief Prevatte who had already heard from the highway patrol about Jimmy Spivey. He was ecstatic, thanked Jake profusely, and said he owed him one.

His last call was to the Farmers and they were also delighted with the news. Jake assured them he would keep them informed of any more developments.

The drive back to Ocean Isle went quickly with

Jake being pleased with himself and filling the late afternoon with songs causing Sandy to watch him with a questioning look. She had not seen Jake so happy in a long time. She put her head in his lap and endured his singing.

CHAPTER 13

BACK AT THE CABIN

SUNDAY APRIL 7, 2003

The mountain air was much fresher than the coastal air and a little chillier, but Jake realized he really enjoyed both environments. When he unlocked the gate he noticed some footprints in the soft sand that he had put on both sides of the gate. He was careful not to disturb them and made a mental note to check them out later.

As he drove up the drive, he couldn't tell that anything had been disturbed, but he was very careful when he got out of his truck. Sandy was not so careful and bounded out as soon as the door was open. She seemed glad to be back home. Jake missed Barbara's having the house all nice and ready for him when he returned from a trip.

Everything was just as he had left it. In a few minutes the heat had taken the chill out of the air and Jake had fed Sandy and put her back outside. He checked the alarm system to be sure it was on. He called the sheriff's office and informed them that he was back in town.

The sun was setting and it was nice to hear the rushing of Reams Creek again. Not the sound of the ocean, but it sure was soothing.

Sandy scratched at the door and Jake let her back in and she plopped down in her bed, letting him know that she was back in her right place.

It was not long until all the mountain sounds lulled Jake and Sandy both to sleep.

Jake slept in longer than he had expected and just as he was getting out of bed, his road alarm went off and he was relieved to see a patrol car coming up the drive.

It was Ken. Jake met him at the back door.

"What brings you out so early?"

"Got your message that you were back in town and just wanted to check in with you. Everything all right?"

"Some footprints out by the gate, but I haven't had a chance to check them out yet. Probably nothing, but with John Wesley on the loose again I can't be too careful."

"Heard you have already apprehended one of the thugs that killed that fellow at the beach. They might have to put you back on the payroll."

"No way. That was just a streak of good luck. The other one is still out there, but they should have him shortly. His partner will probably rat him out if he did not shoot the guy. What's up with you?"

"Been itching to get on the trout waters. You interested?"

"Sure, I just need a day or two around here to catch up on some chores and I'll be ready to go."

"I'll give you a call tomorrow and we will plan a trip to the high country."

"Sounds great. Look forward to it."

Jake fed Sandy, got his own breakfast and then went to the post office and picked up his mail. There was nothing there, but an Orvis catalogue, which made the upcoming trip a little more interesting. A postcard from his folks indicated that they were having a wonderful time on their cruise and said they would call when they returned.

Back at the cabin he walked around the perimeter and checked to see if he could tell whether anyone had been around. No sign of anyone. but he did notice that the deer had been eating his shrubs. Now that Sandy was back and marking her territory maybe the deer wouldn't be so free to come into his yard. Even though Jake loved to see them, he did not like having his shrubbery mowed off at the ground.

His cell phone rang and it was John.

"You back in your part of heaven?" John asked.

"Yeah, Sandy and I are enjoying being back and spring is just waiting to burst forth. Can't wait until all the laurel and rhododendron are in bloom. What's happening with you?"

"Just wanted to let you know that this case at the beach is about wrapped up. We were with JAG yesterday and picked up Sam McLean after Jimmy Spivey made a deal and ratted him out. Looks like Sam was the shooter. The chief of course is glad it is over and he was there to help locate Sam and take credit for the good police work that enabled them to catch the two thugs so quickly. We also informed the Farmers out of courtesy to you. Barbara and I'll be heading back to DC in the morning. She had so much fun on your train trip down to the state fair that she talked me into taking the train back up to DC since we were already in Fayetteville. We decided not to tell Malcolm until we get back to the office."

"Well, that sounds great. Were you able to determine if these two were working alone or whether someone else was involved?"

"The other fellow, and the brains behind it, was Simon Britt. He was a shady lawyer there in Fayetteville and was just trying to get rich quick, but did not mean for anyone to get hurt. The other two got too carried away. When Sergeant Farmer wouldn't give them the information they wanted, they had a struggle and he saw their faces, so they thought the only way out was to kill him."

"Glad it is all over. Ken came out this morning and we are going trout fishing. I'll be away from the cabin for a few days. We are going to fish Wilson Creek over near Grandfather Mountain. Been a long time since I have been over there and I am really looking forward to it. It is such beautiful country."

"Aren't you the lucky one? I'd like it all except the camping out. The army cured me of sleeping on the ground as long as there is still a bed left in the world."

"Well it will be just for a couple of nights and a good air mattress eliminates all the sticks and stones in your back."

"Have fun and I'll talk to you when you get back."

Jake put his phone away and began to make mental notes of what he needed to get together for his trip. It had been a while since he had been fishing and the last time he had looked, his gear needed tending to. Jake had told Ken that he would look after the food if Ken would look after what fishing flies would work for this time of year on Wilson Creek. Ken was much more up on this than Jake was.

Sandy must have felt the excitement because she came over and started following Jake around, nosing into each thing that Jake got out to pack. In a little while he had all his clothes out and hung the sleeping bag outside to air out since it had not been used in a while. He pumped up his air mattress to check that it was still good. He had a flashback to the last time he had used it. He and Jackie had spent three days backpacking on the Appalachian Trail in the Shenandoah Valley. A tear rolled down his cheek and he wiped it away with the back of his hand. Those were good memories and he missed Jackie very much.

Back to reality, he took out a note pad and made a grocery list. He would buy things for breakfast and lunch, but they would depend on the fish they caught for supper. His cooking gear was in a box in the shed. He and Ken had decided against using the Coleman Stove and had concluded they would enjoy cooking over the open fire. The Dutch oven and reflector oven would provide them some good deserts and bread. Ken had told him that there was still enough old dead chestnut wood in this remote area to provide plenty of firewood.

He was surprised at how quickly he was packed and ready to go. Sandy continued to follow him around. There was no way she was going to let him leave her.

On his way to the grocery store he called Ken and confirmed their plans. They would leave early in the morning and stay three days if the fishing warranted it.

"Jake, here is something you should consider. The park regulations require that you keep Sandy on a leash at all times and I know that wouldn't be pleasant for her. I suggest that you leave her at the cabin and one of the deputies who will be checking on your place anyway could feed her and spend a little time with her each day and put her inside at night. They like your place even though they liked it better when Barbara was there."

"I appreciate the offer, and let me think about it. Sandy seems all geared up to go, but keeping her on a leash is not one of her favorite things and I certainly don't want to put you in a bad situation by not obeying the law."

On the way back from the grocery store Jake reasoned that it would be better if Sandy stayed at the cabin. He hated to leave her, but that probably would be the best thing to do.

CHAPTER 14

THE WILSON CREEK TRIP

MONDAY APRIL 8, 2003

At seven the next morning the alarm sounded and Jake saw Ken's truck come up the drive. He met him at the back door and Sandy pushed between them to get her petting.

"You ready to hit the road?" Ken asked.

"Sure am. You want any coffee?"

"No, I am good to go. Let me help you get your stuff into the truck."

Ken quizzed him about a few things to be sure they had everything they needed. Jake fed Sandy and told her he would be back shortly. Sandy watched with a sad face as the truck left the cabin and went down the drive. Jake looked back and wished in his heart he could take her, but he knew leaving her at the cabin was the best thing to do.

"How are we going?" Jake asked, trying to forget about leaving Sandy.

"There are several ways, but the way I prefer is to turn off the Blue Ridge Parkway at milepost 311.1. That will put us on Old Jonas Ridge Road. I call it the scenic route."

"Sounds great to me. Looking forward to getting into the stream and getting my fly caught up in some overhanging branches."

They both laughed and knew it was likely to happen since Jake had not been fishing in a while.

"Won't take you long to get back into the hang of it. I have seen you fish and you know what you are doing, but make no mistake, I'll bring out the largest fish."

"Says who?" Jake said, slapping him on the shoulder.

"Hey, be careful of my fishing arm," Ken said as he turned onto the forest service road.

They passed a Christmas tree farm on the right and a little white church on the left. The main road curved to the right, then continued straight past the church onto a narrower forest service road. Jake was amazed at how beautiful it was as they continued to follow the creek. They talked about the flies they should use as they bounced along on the forest service road. Ken told Jake that he had a good variety of flies including cooper John's, Mercer's micro mayflies, pheasant tails, squirmy wormies, Chec nymphs, Hise's ooey gooey grubs, along with black, olive or white woolly buggers.

"You are not holding out some special fly so you can be sure to catch the largest fish, are you?" Jake asked laughingly.

"Not sure I need to when I am fishing with a flatllander like you," Ken replied jokingly.

They were now in Grandfather District of the Pisgah Forest, which was added to the National Wild and Scenic River Systems in 2000. Wilson creek stretched twenty-three miles before it emptied into John's River and they continued on unpaved forest service roads that followed the creek gorge until they came to Mortimer Recreation Area.

"There are easier ways to get here, but I wanted you to see the beauty of this area since you had not been here in a while," Ken said to Jake.

"We passed a lot of nice fishing holes. Every time I thought I saw the nicest one the next one looked even better. I am loving it."

"Think we should set up camp before we hit the stream in case the weather turns bad on us?"

"Makes sense to me."

There was no one else in the camping area and they drove through until they found a nice high spot near the toilet facilities. In just a few minutes they had the tent set up and everything in its place. Jake tried his cell phone, but couldn't get any reception.

"I meant to warn you about the reception up here," Ken said.

"There is no one I have to talk to, but what about you?" Jake asked.

"I am glad to be away from it, but the dispatcher knows she can reach me through the Forest Service if it is an emergency."

They put on their waders, which would help protect them from the icy April waters and then took the short trail to the creek. Jake went upstream and Ken went downstream.

"The first fish of any size means the other person cooks supper," Ken yelled as he made his first perfect cast into an eddy of the fast moving stream.

"You're on," Jake yelled back as his first cast bounced his fly off a rock into a nice big pool.

"Fish on," Ken yelled followed by a loud "darn" as the fish managed to get away.

Jake had a strike, but no fish and then Ken yelled in glee, as he was able to land the first fish.

"Just three more and we will have something for you to cook for supper," Ken yelled at a dejected Jake.

They continued to banter back and forth as they moved around on the stream. Ken had certainly picked out some productive flies Jake thought.

They had been is such a hurry to get on the water and the fish were so responsive that they both forgot about having their lunch until late in the afternoon. They got back together and sat on a large rock in the middle of the stream and ate a candy bar and talked about what a fabulous time they were having. As they parted ways again to continue their fishing, they agreed to keep two fish each to have for supper.

The sun was beginning to set when Jake joined Ken back at the campsite. Ken had gathered some firewood and started a fire. Jake gathered up the four nice fish, a filet knife, a pan, a plastic bag to put the fish remains in, and went off to clean the day's catch. By the time he got back Ken had gotten out the other things they needed for supper and while the fish were frying, Jake made a little slaw and fried some cornbread in the other skillet. The pot of coffee was already boiling as the two hungry men filled their plates and sat by the fire to devour their tasty meal.

"Nothing quite like fresh fish cooked over an open fire, is there Jake?"

"Even if I had not been starved, this would have been great." Jake responded.

As the pie baked in the Dutch oven, they sipped their coffee and talked about the big fish that got away. After finishing their pie, the evening grew longer and the fish tales got bigger. They decided it was time for bed when they began to catch each other nodding off during the fish tales.

CHAPTER 15

BAD NEWS

MONDAY, APRIL 7, 2003

Ken and Jake had been on the water for several hours when they heard a horn honking up on the road by their truck.

They had gone several miles upstream from the camp and wondered who would be trying to contact them. Their cell phones were not getting any signal so they had been out of contact with anyone since they had gotten to the campground.

Ken and Jake started toward the trail back to the road. They both had caught and released several nice fish and Jake remarked to Ken when he caught him on the trail, "You picked some good flies. The fish have been hitting almost everything I put out there."

As they neared the road, Ken recognized Vern

Gonski, the district ranger for this part of the forest where they were.

"Hello Vern, what brings you up here?"

" I thought that this was your truck, but I was not sure. Glad I found you. Is this Jake?"

"Sure is," Jake responded.

"Ken, your officer called early this morning and I have some bad news for Jake. Someone broke into his cabin last night and took Sandy with them. They left a ransom note for Jake telling him that they would give Sandy back if he gave their money back to them."

"They had better not hurt Sandy. That SOB has already killed my wife," Jake shouted out loud as he hit his hat on his pants leg.

"We had better go pack up and get back and see what we can do," Ken said, trying to calm Jake down.

"Sorry to have been the bearer of bad news," Vern said to them both.

"Appreciate your tracking us down," Jake said.

"Please contact my office and tell them I am on my way back in," Ken told Vern.

Ken and Jake threw their gear in the back of the pickup and rode back to the campsite in silence. Ken felt the pain he knew Jake was feeling, but did not know anything to say that he thought would comfort him.

In a few minutes they had all their gear back in Ken's truck, but not as neat and orderly as it had been packed for the trip out.

As they left the campground Jake finally said,

"I have one ace in the hole they don't know about. As a puppy in DC, Sandy kept trying to escape out of her pen and we had a chip imbedded under her skin. There is also one in her collar, but they probably figured that out and threw it away. I can find her. I just hope it is in time."

Ken was back on the main road pretty quickly and it was not long before they were nearing Asheville. Ken contacted his office as soon as he was able to, but they did not have much information to give him. The cabin had been broken into and searched, but it did not appear that anything was missing except Sandy. Through fingerprints they had confirmed that John Wesley Williams had been in the cabin with another person who they had not identified yet. There was a note that told Jake to contact them and get the money ready if Jake wanted to see Sandy alive again.

"Jake, let us handle this and we will get Sandy back for you."

"I have to be involved. I can't let anything happen to her. As soon as I get to the cabin, I'll get the trace set up and try to find out where she is. I am not going to give them any money and if they mess with me very much, you will not have to worry about holding them for trial. If they hurt Sandy, their life want be worth a plug nickel."

"I know exactly how you feel, but it might be better if you did not say anything to me about it. I do not want to perjure myself if it comes down to a trial."

"I certainly understand; I do not want to put you into the middle of this. You have to stick to the law and I appreciate that."

"I am going to call the office and send the guys who can trace phone calls out to your place so we will be ready to move when you are."

In his mind, Jake was going through the procedure of how to track Sandy on his computer. If he couldn't get it to work he would get in touch with his dad who would be able to make it work.

As they turned into Jake's driveway a deputy's vehicle was already there and they were taking equipment into the cabin.

Jake had hoped that this was just a bad dream and that Sandy would be running out to meet Ken's truck, but there was no Sandy to greet him and he had to wipe away a tear.

As they entered the cabin, the two deputies spoke to them and said they were almost ready with the equipment to try to trace any phone calls.

Jake's cell phone rang just as he entered the den and the deputies looked worried because they were not quite ready and they were preparing to put the trace on the land line. Jake quieted their fears by telling them it was Barbara on the phone.

"Hello, Barbara."

"Jake, what is happening? We just got word that John Wesley has broken into your cabin and taken Sandy and is holding her for ransom. Malcolm says we have to get John Wesley Williams back in prison. John and I are on our way on the first flight out to Asheville. "

"Y'all are welcome to stay at my place."

"We'll see what time we get there. I know what Sandy means to you, but don't go off and do something stupid."

"I am going to get her back and I just hope no one gets in my way. Ken and his crew will keep me out of trouble until you get here," Jake said smiling at Ken and his deputies.

Jake hung up the phone and plopped down in the chair in front of his computer. When he got it up and running, he pulled a flash drive out of the drawer and plugged it in. In a few minutes a map showed up on the screen with a little red dot that was moving back and forth.

"I found her and she is moving around," Jake yelled out loud to Ken and his deputies.

They all rushed over to the computer screen. Jake enhanced the map on the screen and everyone was looking trying to make out where it was.

"Looks like it is the old warehouse district down by the French Broad River where there are a lot of vacant buildings," Ken said.

"They must have her tied up. She is pacing back and forth which means she is all right," Jake said.

"Now that we know she is all right, we should make the call to see what they want you to do," Ken said.

"Are you fellows ready to try to get the trace?" Jake asked.

"Yes, we are all set up. Try to keep them talking as long as you can. I'll signal you when we get a sure location."

Jake went to his telephone and dialed the number on the ransom note. The phone rang several times and then a voice said, "Yes."

"This is Jake Johnson and I think you have something I want."

"Well, you have something I want," the voice on the other end of the telephone replied.

"What do I have that you want? You have my dog."

"You have my $600,000 and I want it all back."

"Who is this? I don't have that kind of money."

"You found it in the mountains and have deposited it in an off shore account and it belongs to me and if you want to see your dog alive you will give it back to me."

"I didn't find any money and I don't have $600,000. You have to come up with something more realistic than that."

"Don't play games with me. Here is what you do. At 10 a.m. you bring the money to Hemphill Knob Road off the Blue Ridge Parkway. Go beyond the building to the end of the road. There will be a blue Ford Mustang in the parking lot. Place the bag with the money on the front seat and leave the area. I'll know when you are back out on the Parkway. Drive back toward Asheville. When I have the money and have left this area I'll call you and you can come get your dog."

"No way, man. I am not going to give you any

money until I know that Sandy is all right."

"No money and you can fish her out of the river in an old fertilizer sack. Drive your old red pickup and if we see any sign of cops, the deal is off and the dog goes swimming."

Jake let his emotions get the better of him and he blurted out, "You hurt one hair on Sandy and all the money in the world will not be able to protect you. I'll track you down and then no one will have to worry about bringing you to trial again or putting you back in prison."

Ken put his hand on Jake's shoulder to calm him down and about that time the deputy gave them a thumbs up that he had established a location for the call.

"Give me the money and you will never see me again and your precious dog will be back home chasing rabbits real soon. Tomorrow at 10 a.m. Don't be late."

Jake heard the click as the phone went dead.

"The call came from the parking lot at the airport. It was a cell phone and now that we have this information we can track it if he makes any more calls."

Jake checked the computer and the little red dot was still pacing back and forth.

"Let's go get Sandy now before they know we have located her."

"Not yet, we need to formulate a plan to get Sandy and also to get these guys in the process," Ken said.

"If she is in the same place in the morning, we can get her and get the thugs all at the same time. Ten a.m. should give us plenty of time to work out all the details. Let's ride up to the parkway and check out the area. Pretty sure they both won't come. John Wesley will send his henchman so we need to have a plan in place to get all the way back to him."

Ken and Jake took an unmarked police car and went up on the parkway. They turned onto Hemphill Knob road and went to the end of the road past all the buildings. They were surprised to find that the blue Mustang was already in the parking lot. Using his cell phone, Jake took some pictures of the car and the adjoining area without being obvious.

"After dark I'll send an officer up here to put a tracking device on that car even thought I do not think they will use it other than as a drop spot," Ken said to Jake.

"It is really strange that he picked the Ranger Headquarters for his drop-off point. Let's go talk to the ranger and maybe he will have some suggestions how to tail these guys while they are on the parkway," Jake said to Ken.

They stopped in the visitor's spot in front of the Headquarters building and went inside.

Ken introduced himself to the receptionist and asked to see the ranger in Charge. She paged Ranger Simpson and Ken recognized him as soon as he appeared. They had worked on some law enforcement assignments together in the past, but Ken did not realize that Simpson was the head ranger in this district.

"Good to see you again Ken," Ranger Simpson said to Ken as he shook his hand."

"I did not realize that you were the head ranger," Ken said as he introduced Simpson to Jake.

"Well, I just got the promotion in the last couple of months so I am pretty new to this job. What brings you up here?"

Ken related the whole story of John Wesley Williams and what was presently taking place. Ranger Simpson listened with interest.

"What can we do to help?"

"We need to let these fellows think they are getting away with it so we can hopefully get back to John Wesley. We do not want to spook them, but we can't afford to loose contact with them either. What is the best way to tail them on the parkway?"

"With Spring about here, the traffic is picking up, but the limited access should help us determine when he leaves the parkway. I agree with you I do not think he will use the Mustang. We had not picked up on the fact that a strange car was parked in the utility parking lot. For the past couple of weeks we have had routine checkpoints along the parkway, trying to encourage tourists to buy the National Park sticker that provides free access to all of the national parks. We can have one going on each side of Hemphill Knob Road so they can't leave the parkway without stopping at one of the checkpoints. We can put surveillance on the

Mustang so we will know what kind of car recovers the money from the drop spot. When they are stopped on the parkway, one of our officers can place a tracking device on the car that will trace them no matter where they go after that. One thing I just thought of is that our shifts change at 10:30 and that will mean a lot of cars coming and going in here. He is smarter than we give him credit for. If we work our plan we can still identify their car and track it where ever it goes."

"That sounds like a workable plan," Ken said as he looked at Jake and they both nodded their heads in agreement.

Ranger Simpson called in two other rangers and they discussed the plan and worked out the details about how the personnel would be deployed.

The phone rang. Ranger Simpson listened for a minute and then hung up the phone.

"The Mustang is a stolen car reported missing two days ago so they have had this plan for a while. We have put a tracking device on the mustang in case they surprise us and use it as the getaway vehicle."

"Looks like you are covering all the bases," Jake said.

"We appreciate your help and will see you in the morning," Ken said shaking Ranger Simpson's hand as they left the room.

As they left the building and got in the car, Ken said, "Now we have to go fix up a money bag drop."

"If they see it is not real they will abort the plan

and we will have no chance of getting to Williams."

"They will think it is real and you probably will not be able to tell the difference. We have a stack of counterfeit bills that I have gotten permission to use."

"That should do the trick. Do you have someone who would pass for me? I want to go get Sandy while this is going on so we will be sure we have her even if something goes wrong with our getting to Williams."

"Yeah, but we will need your pickup. I'll have an officer go with you and you can use one of our vehicles. But we want to be sure this is underway before you go in case Williams is with Sandy."

"If he is, I'll take care of him."

"Don't say things like that. I don't want to have to perjure myself if I ever am put on the stand at your trial for killing him." Ken said with a smirk on his face.

"I'll keep my thoughts to myself," Jake said to pacify Ken.

Back at the office, Ken talked to the officers who would be on the stakeout and also the one going with Jake. After Ken was satisfied that everyone understood what was going to happen he said to Jake," Lets go get some supper. Ruth is expecting you to join us. She said for me not to take no for an answer."

"You do not have to twist my arm. Let's go, I am starved."

On the way to Ken's house they made small

talk as Ken tried to keep Jake's mind off Sandy and what could happen.

Ruth greeted Jake at the door with a big hug and a kiss on the cheek. "Good to see you again, Jake. We have missed having you around. Hope you are hungry."

"I sure am. I have missed seeing you and Ken, but I have been busy at Ocean Isle beach."

"Yes, I hear how you have cleared up the crime wave down there all by yourself."

"Well, that is not exactly the way it happened, but I am glad that it is over. Don't like things to interfere with the serenity of the beach. You and Ken are going to have to come down."

"That would be lovely if I can ever drag him away from his work. The fishing trip with you is the only time he has taken off in a long time. Sorry it got cut short."

"We had a great time while it lasted, but now we have to get Sandy back."

"I am sure you will. She will be back safe and sound in no time at all. Y'all wash up and I'll put supper on the table."

When Jake returned, the table was set with flowers in the centerpiece. Dinner was a big pot roast covered in vegetables and a basket of hot biscuits accompanied by strawberry freezer jam. He noticed a blueberry pie sitting on the stove."

"Ruth you have outdone yourself again. I have not seen such good looking food since I was here last."

"Hush your mouth and sit and let's eat."

Ken and Ruth kept the conversation moving and away from thoughts about Sandy. Ruth kept his glass filled with sweet tea and insisted that he keep eating, but all the while telling him to keep room for the blueberry pie. She had learned that it was his favorite.

They finally pushed back from the table and went to sit in easy chairs in the den. Ruth joined them just about the time they were both about to go to sleep. She livened up the conversation by asking about Barbara and getting Jake to talk about what had been happening with him.

Ken glanced at his watch and said, "I need to check in at the office and to get you back to your place. We had better go. Ruth, do you want to ride with us?"

"No. I'll stay here and finish up with the kitchen. Jake, I have fixed you a plate to carry home with you and I am going to give you the rest of the pie. Neither Ken nor I need anything like that around."

"That is very nice of you and I certainly am not going to refuse."

Jake gave her a big hug and thanked her for the wonderful meal as he and Ken left.

"Let me go by the office and see that everything is set for tomorrow and then I'll run you back out to your cabin. We can exchange vehicles so we will have your truck to make the money drop in the morning. My officer will be at you place about nine and you can be in place at ten to pick up

Sandy. Will your laptop run the program to keep tabs on Sandy?"

"Yeah, we can be in place near the old warehouse so we can move in at ten."

At the office, Ken checked with the officers on duty to see that everything was ready and then he showed Jake the case with the counterfeit money.

"If they happen to get away from us, will they be able to use this money?"

"If they did, it would leave a trail and we probably would be able to find them, but we are not going to let that happen."

"Doesn't look like John and Barbara are going to make it in time to be in on the fun. Their plane does not get in until twelve noon," Jake said.

"Hope we will have it wrapped up by the time they get here. Are you going to pick them up at the airport?"

"Yes, if I am available."

The night was beautiful with the mountains bathed in the bright light of the moon as they drove out Reams Creek Road to Jake's cabin. They saw a small herd of deer in the meadow at Vance's birthplace and Ken slowed down to be sure none of them darted out in front of the car.

"I love to see them, but they sure are a nuisance on the highway," Ken said.

"I have given up on having any pretty shrubs at the cabin, but I still love to see them in the yard."

"I want to check and see if Sandy is still in the same place," Ken said as they pulled up the driveway to Jake's cabin.

"Sure, come on in," Jake said.

Inside the cabin Jake powered up the computer and brought up the surveillance program and the little green light was still in the same location.

"Looks like she is still there. That is good news. She is going to be all right. They would have done something with her by now if that was their plan," Ken said.

"I think you are right," Jake said.

'I'll not see you in the morning, but I'll keep in touch by telephone," Ken said as he went out the door to return home.

Jake prepared for bed knowing that it would be a long night and that he wouldn't get much rest thinking about Sandy and hoping everything was going to work out to get her back. He was concerned about their catching Williams, but not as much as he was about getting his companion back safe and sound. She meant so much to him and in a way she was his link to Jackie, his wife, who had given her to Jake as a very small puppy.

The whippoorwills and the rushing of Reams Creek were soothing sounds and Jake finally went to sleep.

CHAPTER 16

GOOD NEWS

THURSDAY, APRIL 10, 2003

After a very fretful night with little sleep, Jake arose with the sun. He was anxious to get on with it and get Sandy back home safe and sound. He checked to see that she still showed up on the surveillance video, ate his breakfast, and waited for the deputy to arrive. He watched three deer come into his yard and nibble on his grass and shrubs. He knew that if Sandy had been there she would have tried to run them off. He did not think that nine o'clock would ever come.

The alarm finally sounded and as he looked out the window, he saw the deputy drive up the driveway. He greeted him at the back door and saw that it was Deputy Simpson.

"Good morning Sam. Are you ready to go get

Sandy."

"I sure am, but Ken reminded me again that we are not to move on it until we get the word from him."

"I understand perfectly, but we can be in place and ready to go. Do you want any coffee before we go?"

"No thanks, I have a thermos in the car."

"Let me get my laptop and we will be on our way. I have it all charged up."

In a few minutes they were parked a block away from the old warehouse on the river, waiting for a call from Ken. Sam knew that Jake was anxious and he made small talk trying to set him at ease. Right after ten the phone rang. Ken said the drop had been made and for them to proceed to get Sandy.

When Jake checked his computer again he almost panicked.

"Sandy is moving away from the warehouse; let's move," He barked at Sam.

As they came near the warehouse, Sam and Jake stared in amazement. A young boy was leading Sandy down the street away from the warehouse.

The deputy pulled the car up beside the boy and got out, looking to see if he could spot anyone else in the area.

"What's your name?" Sam asked as he got out of the car.

"Steve. What's wrong, officer?" the boy

asked.

"We just wanted to see your dog," Sam responded as Jake got out of the car and went and hugged Sandy.

"Where did you get the dog?" Jake asked.

"I was playing with some friends around the old warehouses several days ago and a man was tying this dog inside one of the fences. We came over and started petting the dog and he asked if we would like to have the dog. I immediately said yes and he told me that the dog would have to stay here until today at ten and then I could have her. He gave me ten dollars if I would bring her food and water every day, but I was not to tell anyone about her until today. I was so happy to get a dog that I was willing to do anything."

Sam explained that Sandy was Jake's dog, that she had been kidnapped, and that they had just located her.

Jake saw the disappointment in Steve's eyes and the hurt on his face and knew that he had to do something to make it right with the boy.

Sam broke in and asked, "Can you tell us what the man looked like?"

"He was about your size with dark hair and was wearing blue jeans and a blue button-up shirt."

"Was there any kind of car around?"

"There was an old model truck. I think it was blue, but it was so dusty it was hard to tell. I think it was a Dodge."

"Do you remember anything else?"

"No. I was so excited about the dog that I did

not pay much attention to anything else. I never saw him again after that day."

"That was real helpful. Thank you."

"Are either of your parents at home?" Jake asked.

"Yeah. My mom is at home."

"Get in the car and let's go talk to her for a moment."

Steve and Sandy piled in the back seat and Steve blurted out, "She is not going to be too happy with me. I skipped school so I could go get the dog at ten. I was going to go to school as soon as I did that."

"Will she let you have a dog?"

"Yeah, I think so. When I have asked they never came out and just said no. They said they would think about it."

"Maybe I can help," Jake said.

"Steve, what is your last name?"

"Sanders."

"Can you show us where you live?" Sam said as he cranked the car and started to drive in the direction Steve was walking.

"Sure. Just go to the next corner and turn right."

They drove out of the old warehouse district and into an old neighborhood of well-kept modest homes.

"I live in the green house on the right in the next block," Steve said.

Sam parked the car in front of the house and

they all got out and walked up to the house.

"Go get your mom," Sam said to Steve.

Sam, Jake, and Sandy waited on the porch while Steve went into the house and returned in a few minutes with his mom.

As they came out on the porch, she was asking Steve, "What in the world are you into that the Deputy Sheriff brought you home? Your dad is going to tan your hide."

"Mrs. Sanders, I am Deputy Wilson and this is Jake Johnson and the dog is Sandy. Steve has been helping us rescue Sandy, who was stolen from Jake."

At that moment Sam's phone rang and he stepped off the porch to answer it.

Jake said to Mrs. Sanders, "I would like to take Steve down to the dog pound and get him a dog. He was such a big help in looking after Sandy and helping me get her back that I want to do something for him. I'll take care of all the expenses."

Ms. Sanders looked down at Steve and put her arm around him and said, "I reckon so. His dad and I have talked about it, but we just have not gotten around to it. He has been pestering us to get him a dog for a long time."

"That's great. We will take him back to school just as soon as we get this done."

At the pound, it did not take Steve very long to pick out a cute, playful German Shepherd puppy that met with Jake and Sam's approval. They filled out the necessary paperwork and made arrangements for the proper shots. When Mrs. Sanders saw the puppy, it was love at first sight. Then they took one happy little boy to school and explained to the teacher what had happened.

Sam reported to the sheriff that all was taken care of on their end and asked what was happening with the money drop.

CHAPTER 17

WHAT HAPPENED TO THE MONEY?

THURSDAY, APRIL 10, 2003

At 10 a.m. an officer impersonating Jake drove Jake's truck to the back of the parking lot. He got out carrying a silver case and put it in the parked Mustang. The handle had been altered and a tracking device inserted. The officer drove away as he had been instructed.

Since it was shift-changing time, there were cars coming and going. A park service SUV stopped beside the Mustang and a person wearing a hooded sweatshirt covering his head got out of his vehicle and into the Mustang. Inside, he opened the silver case and checked the money. He then poured the money into a pillowcase and placed a manila envelope inside the silver case.

He returned to the SUV and drove away. The

officer who had been watching the scene reported the license plate to officers at the two checkpoints and indicated that it was a Park Service vehicle.

Ranger Simpson ordered the officers at the two checkpoints to let the vehicle through, but to put a tracking device on the vehicle when it stopped.

The SUV driver turned south on the parkway and in a couple of miles saw the checkpoint. As he pulled up to the checkpoint, the driver said, "Taking the vehicle to be serviced."

"Go ahead," the office said, but not before his partner could place the tracking device on the rear bumper.

The officers radioed Ranger Simpson that the vehicle had gone through the check point and was heading south on the parkway with an unmarked car following.

After another mile, the SUV pulled off the side of the road. The man got out carrying the pillowcase, walked across the road, and was picked up by a car going North on the parkway. The trailing car radioed Ranger Simpson about the transfer. The checkpoint had been disbanded when the SUV had gone through, so there was no way to get another tracking device on the new car.

Ranger Simpson radioed the helicopter that it was now up to them to keep the vehicle in sight until they could get another car in pursuit.

Ranger Mann in the helicopter radioed that he had the vehicle in sight and it was heading north on the parkway. Sheriff Edwards scurried to get a vehicle in place to take over the job of following the crook. Deputies had been placed at various intersections of the parkway for just such an emergency.

Jake and Deputy Simpson were following the progress through the radio, so they headed in the direction of the parkway to see if they could be of any help.

The sheriff reminded all the officers that they were not to make contact with the vehicle, but were just to keep it in sight so they could follow it back to John Wesley Williams' place.

When the car turned off the parkway, there was an unmarked police car in place to take up the pursuit and the helicopter backed off so the crook would not know he was being followed. The vehicle was now on Highway 694 heading back to Asheville. This information allowed the sheriff to contact more deputies who could follow the car without arousing suspicion. The driver of the vehicle made some turns and stops to be sure he was not being followed, but there were enough different law enforcement vehicles that kept changing off, that he did not recognize he was under surveillance.

Jake and Deputy Simpson arrived in the area in order to be close enough to get into the rotation as the crook's car approached downtown Asheville.

After several more turns, stops and pauses the vehicle finally precedes to the American Motel where the driver got out and went into room 23 at the rear of the motel. By this time several cars were in the vicinity and Ken told them all to hold back. He sent a plainclothes deputy into the motel office to find out who had registered for the room where the driver went.

"Sheriff, the room is registered to a Toby Canady from Little Rock and there has not been any other person in the room, according to the clerk."

"OK, run the information to see what you can find out. We will sit tight until he makes a move."

While they were waiting Jake and the deputy arrived on the scene and got into Ken's car.

"What's happening?" Jake asked.

"Waiting to check out some information," Ken replied.

"Well, Sandy is safe and sound and we have made one little boy very happy. Will give you the details later."

The radio squawked on and the deputy said, "No record of a Toby Canady in Little Rock and the rest of the information doesn't check out either."

"OK, go get our man and let's see what is happening."

As the deputy emerged from the office, two cars pulled into the parking lot. Four deputies got out and two went to the front door and two went to where they could see the back of the motel.

With guns drawn, the two at the front knocked on the door and identified themselves as police. The door opened and the man inside asked, "What is going on?"

"Please step outside," the officer replied.

The man came outside and one of the officers went inside and emerged in a moment, saying, "No one else is in the room."

By this time Ken, had arrived on the scene and asked, "Where is the pillowcase with the money?"

"What money?"

"The money you took out of the Ford Mustang at the Ranger headquarters."

"You have the wrong person. I do not have any money."

"Why are you registered under a phony name?"

"I am trying to hide from my wife, that's why."

"We know you are the man that took the ransom money from the car because we have trailed you all the way back here. Impound his vehicle and take him back to the office for questioning. Get the lab boys to go over the car and this room. That money has to be somewhere. Also, pick up the Ford Mustang and take it to the impound lot for the lab boys."

Jake had remained out of sight. When they took the man away, he came up to talk to Ken, who had looked in the room and was puzzled about where the money could be.

"I am going to call the number I have and ask to get Sandy back now that he has the money. I am not going to let him know that we have Sandy back. We want to make him think I am still after him to get her back."

"Sounds like a good idea to me. Let's wait

until we get back to the office so we can try to get a location from his telephone. Simpson stay here and secure the room. Jake can go with me," Ken said.

Jake got Sandy out of Simpson's car and Ken took a moment to pet and talk to her before he got in his car.

"She does not look any worse for wear," Ken said.

"The kid taking care of her did a good job. He was disappointed that he did not get to keep her, but we got him a nice dog that he can grow up with."

Jake told Ken the whole story as they went back to the office.

"Still trying to figure out how these fellows gave us the slip. There had to be a third guy involved. One of them got out of the car while we were tailing them without our knowing about it. They were pretty slick. They knew that we would have a tail on them. We were looking after the car, not thinking about how many people were in it. We can't let them get away with our counterfeit money."

Back at the office, they set up the phones to trace the call. Then Jake made the call.

"You have your money and now I want Sandy back."

"I told you no cops and they were swarming all over the place. Forget about getting your precious dog back. Someone will fish her dead body out of the river."

"I told you what would happen if you harmed her. You better be watching your back because I am going to show up when you least expect it and the police will not have to worry about you anymore. If they ever find you at all."

"I'm not worried. I'll be kicking back somewhere spending my well- deserved money."

"You never did fulfill your obligations for the money and even though you won't reveal who hired you, he will come looking for you because you got part of the money before you finished the job."

"Oh well, you can't please everyone, but maybe I'll decide to finish the job, so you had better be on your toes."

"I'll end up finding you and who hired you, and will put an end to this mess. I'm not in the FBI anymore so I will have free rein when I find you both. Oh by the way, the money you have so cleverly gotten is counterfeit so when you leave us a trail of counterfeit bills you will be an easy target.

I knew you wouldn't keep your end of the bargain about returning Sandy, so I definitely was not going to give you any money. Be sure to pay your accomplices with the counterfeit money so we can track them down also."

The phone on the other end went dead and Jake shook his head and asked, "Did we get a trace?"

"It was a cell phone and it was in the vicinity of the airport."

Ken said, "Dispatch, send a car to the airport to see if they can spot our man."

"What do we do now?" Jake asked.

Before Ken could answer, in walked Barbara

and John.

"Well, look who is here," Ken said.

"Are we too late for all the fun?" Barbara asked.

"No, you are just in time to help track down John Wesley Williams again," Jake said as he went over and gave Barbara a big hug and a kiss on the cheek, and then shook John's hand and gave him a hug.

"We have managed to let him get away with our ransom money," Ken said.

"What about Sandy?" Barbara asked.

"She is fine. We got her back with no trouble and they do not know that we have her. They had given her to a little boy, but we found her and now the little boy has a new dog," Jake said.

"Any clue as to where Williams might be?" John asked.

"Our last contact put him near the airport so we might have lost him. We are checking to see if he is trying to fly out. We should go out there and give my deputies a hand in trying to locate him," Ken said.

"I'll check on any private planes," John said as he left the room to start making calls.

"Do your deputies know what he looks like?" Barbara asked as the three of them left the building to go to the airport.

"We have distributed pictures, so I hope they will recognize him. Don't think he is into disguises and I don't think he was expecting us to be so close on his tail."

When they reached the airport, Ken contacted his deputies who were patrolling the terminal, but they had not seen anyone who even resembled John Wesley Williams.

Barbara checked with the desk to see what flights were going out and to see the list of passengers. A flight to Vegas was in the process of boarding and as she checked the list, she found a John Wesley on the manifest.

Barbara and Jake explained to the airport officials what was happening. Barbara went on the plane to check the passengers who had already boarded. According to the list, John Wesley was not one of them. She stationed herself at the back of the plane, checked the rest rooms, and waited to see what might happen. She called Ken and reported that the plane was clear, but that she would stay there until it was ready to depart.

Jake and Ken kept a close eye on the passengers boarding, but did not see their man anywhere. The rest of the deputies covered the entrances so they had the airport pretty well locked down, but there was no sign of Williams anywhere.

Ken got a report from John that there were no private planes scheduled to leave the airport that day.

After a thorough search of the terminal and hangers, Ken called off the search and the deputies left the airport. Ken, Barbara, and Jake returned to the office to meet with John. After a brief discussion of the day's events, John, Barbara, and Jake decided to call it a day and leave for Jake's cabin. Barbara rode with Jake; John followed with Sandy in the rental car.

CHAPTER 18

PERFECT ALARM SYSTEM

FRIDAY, APRIL 11, 2003

Jake and Barbara enjoyed catching up on what had been happening in their private lives on the ride out to Jake's cabin. Jake stopped at the grocery store and they bought some steaks and fixings for supper.

Barbara really seemed to be happy to be back in the mountain environment, but not as happy as Sandy was to be back in her familiar surroundings.

The three enjoyed their grilled meal and the chance to be together. They appreciated the opportunity to put work behind then for a few minutes. The chilly April evening felt good as they sat around the campfire which Jake had made after they finished their meal.

"Where are the marshmallows?" John inquired.

"Yeah, we can't have a campfire without marshmallows," Barbara chimed in.

Jake took the hint and in a moment he was back with a bag of marshmallows, some chocolate and three coat hangers, saying as he came out the door, "You will have to cook your own."

They sat and ate and talked and listened to the rush of the stream and the night creatures whose sounds contributed to the atmosphere. Sandy was enjoying the attention from Barbara as she rubbed her head and dropped a few marshmallows her way.

When the fire died down, they decided it was time to call it a day.

The phone ringing awakened Jake about seven thirty in the morning, and a cheerful greeting from Ken brought Jake out of the pleasant dream he was having.

"Well, he has slipped through our fingers again. He rented a car and drove to Hickory, where he flew out on a private jet headed for Vegas. We are contacting the authorities there, but he had time to make the trip and get away from the airport before we knew about it."

"I reckon Malcolm will be sending John and Barbara back out there to look for him," Jake replied.

"Are you going?" Ken asked.

"No. I'll let you professionals take it from here.

Sandy and I are going to just take it easy for a few days. I hear John talking on his cell phone so I reckon Malcolm is giving him his marching orders. I'll check in with you later today."

As Jake entered the kitchen, the back door opened and Barbara and Sandy came in from a morning jog.

"Good morning, sleepy head," Barbara quirked to Jake as she got some orange juice from the fridge.

"How was your run?"

"Great. Sandy and I enjoyed it like old times. Not much has changed."

"Looks like Williams has made it out of the state. John has been on the phone with Malcolm already this morning, but I do not know what was said. Ken called and told me what had happened."

"Where is he now?"

"Sounds like he is already back in Vegas."

"Well, I was hoping we could have some more time together, but Malcolm probably wants us back out in Vegas."

John entered the room and said, "You are right. We are to leave as soon as we can. I have called the airport and we have a nine o'clock flight. No rest for the weary."

Jake prepared breakfast as John and Barbara got their things together. It was not long before he and Sandy were saying goodbye to them and watched their car disappear around the curve in the driveway.

Jake puttered around the house, a little sad

that their trip had been cut short and he had not been able to spend any alone time with Barbara. In the early afternoon he decided to take a little run and he and Sandy were enjoying themselves when a light mist started, but it felt good on Jake's face and he continued for another mile before he turned around and started for home. The air was a little fresher up here in the mountains than it was at the coast when he and Sandy enjoyed running on the beach. This gave him some time to think about what he was going to do until his next assignment came along.

Back at the cabin he cleaned up a little and then decided he would go into town for supper. He fed Sandy and left her in the cabin because he was not going to be gone very long. He stopped at BoJangles and had some fried chicken and some sweet ice tea.

He took Sandy for a little walk when he got home and then sat down to watch some TV. Flipping through the channels, he couldn't find anything that sparked his interest and about nine he decided he would turn in.

Around two in the morning, Sandy, who was standing at the window giving a low growl, awakened him from a nice dream about him and Barbara on the beach. Since that was not something Sandy usually did, Jake looked out the window and saw the dark shadow of a man walking up his driveway with a drawn pistol in his hand.

Jake thought, whoever this is knew about the

alarm system and bypassed it as he walked up the drive.

Jake put Sandy in the bathroom and told her to be quiet. He reached for his four-ten shotgun and put his pistol in his belt. By this time he heard someone open his back door. He took his pillows and put them under the cover to look like he was still sleeping and took a position behind the door so he wouldn't be seen when the bedroom door was opened. The floor creaked as the man approached the bedroom and slowly pushed open the door. As he aimed his pistol at the lump in the bed and fired three quick shots, Jake stepped out from behind the door, placed the shotgun in the man's back, and said, "Throw your gun on the bed and don't give me an excuse to shoot you right now. Turn around so I can see who you are. Well! John Wesley, you didn't go to Vegas after all. That was just a ploy to get me off guard."

The man threw the gun on the bed and Jake checked to see that he did not have any other weapons.

"Lay face down on the floor and please don't give me any reason to shoot you other than the fact that you shot my wife and just attempted to kill me. I don't want a hole in my floor and blood on my rug."

Jake went to the closet and took a length of rope from his backpack and tied the man's hands behind his back. After securing Williams, Jake opened the bathroom door and Sandy came out to investigate. The hairs on her neck bristled and she gave a low growl again. In a few minutes she went over to the man, and with her teeth showing she gave another low growl.

"Get this dog off me," Williams yelled."

"You should have treated her better, then she wouldn't dislike you so much. She hardly ever growls, but it was a dead giveaway tonight that something was really wrong. If it had not been for her, those bullets you fired into my bed would probably have been in me."

As the man squirmed, Sandy licked his face.

"Look like she has forgiven you, or, is she just tasting you?" Jake said laughing.

Jake picked up the phone and dialed the sheriff's office.

"This is Jake Johnson. Please send a car out to pick up John Wesley Williams, who just broke into my house and tried to kill me. I have him in custody. Please hurry before he does something I have to shoot him for."

"We will be right there, Jake and will notify Ken that you have him at your house."

"You must have been coming to kill me tonight for the other half of your fee that you never got and I don't believe you ever will. It is a good thing that you decided not to hurt Sandy or my shotgun would have certainly gone off tonight when I saw who was in my house. I am sure the judge is now going to add to your sentence."

Jake heard the sirens in the distance, but they stopped at the head of his driveway. In a few minutes his alarm went off and when he looked out the window, he saw two police cars coming up the driveway.

The officers hurried out of their cars and came into the house as Jake met them at the back door.

"He is back in the bedroom. Sandy is standing guard."

"I have not touched his gun, which is laying on the bed. He put three shots into my bed, thinking I was there.

As they listened to Jake's tale, they replaced the rope with handcuffs, took Williams out to the patrol car, and put him in the back seat.

"He had parked his car at the bottom of the driveway and walked in so he wouldn't turn on your alarm. Guess what we found in the car? The pillowcase with the ransom money still in it."

"Well. I'll be. Glad we got that back. I hated to see all that counterfeit money being used. Ken will certainly be relieved because he hated to tell Malcolm and the FBI that he had lost their $500,000."

As they talked, Ken drove up and came into the house.

"Glad you are alright," He said to Jake.

The deputy was coming from the bedroom where he had taken some pictures, bagged the gun, and dug the slugs out of the mattress.

"Take him into town and lock him up. I'll feel better when I see him behind bars. Have his car towed to the impound lot so the lab boys can go over it. Put that money back into the evidence locker," Ken said to the deputies.

Ken called the office and reported on what had happened and told them to notify Malcolm at the FBI office in Washington.

"Wonder if he will send John and Barbara back here?" Jake asked with a smile on his face.

"If you keep catching all the crooks, they are going to force you to go back to work," Ken said, laughing.

Ken excused himself, saying he had better get back to the office to be sure that nothing happened to John Wesley Williams.

When Ken was gone, Jake called Barbara and said, "Have you heard the news?"

"It had better be something good at this hour," Barbara quipped with a sleepy voice.

"Sorry, I thought you would have been out for your morning jog."

"Don't forget there is a little time difference here."

"Darn. I forgot about that, but the good news is that John Wesley is being transported to the Asheville jail as we speak. He attempted to kill me, but Sandy gave me an early warning and I was ready for him. I'll tell you the whole story later. Go back to sleep."

Jake relaxed in his recliner and Sandy came over and laid her head on his feet.

"Thank you, gal, you saved my life," Jake said as he stroked her head.

The next thing he knew the phone was ringing and it was nine o'clock in the morning.

"Hello."

"Jake, this is John. Glad you are all right. Malcolm has called us back to Washington and is going to get some of the local agents to transport Williams to the Federal Pen. Don't know when we will see you again, but glad all this worked out. Give Sandy a hug for me and I'll give Barbara one for you. Take care."

CHAPTER 19

LET'S START ALL OVER AGAIN

SATURDAY, APRIL 12. 2003

Jake had just hung up the phone when it rang again.

"Hello. This is Jake."

"This is Ken. Bad news, brother, John Wesley is on the loose again. The deputies who were bringing him in to jail stopped at Vance Birthplace on Reams Creek Road to help a couple they thought needed help, and they were two of John Wesley's friends. They got the drop on the deputies, locked them in the back of the patrol car, and got away. They headed toward Weaverville so they probably will not be coming your way, but be careful."

"How did they fool the deputies?"

"It was a man and a woman and the man

156

flagged down the patrol car saying the woman was in labor and that she needed help. One deputy went to the car and the other stayed with the patrol car and called 911 for the EMT's. The other one went to assist the woman and they got the drop on him and then the other man went back to the patrol car and said that the other officer needed help. When he got out of the car and started to go to help, they got the drop on him. That is when they locked them in the car and left. The EM's found them and let them out, but it was too late. We put out an all points bulletin and found their car at a gas station. Now we do not know what kind of vehicle they are in or where they are going."

"Darn. Glad the deputies are all right, but will we ever be able to catch and hold that SOB? Maybe next time if I get him in my sights we won't have to worry about him anymore."

"Calm down, Jake. I do not want you to do anything foolish. We will catch him again and put him away for good. You and Sandy be careful and I will keep in touch."

VISIT TO CARY

CHAPTER 20

MONDAY, APRIL 29, 2003

After several weeks in the mountains, Jake headed back to Ocean Isle for some relaxing on the beach. His parents were just back from their cruise and he went through Cary to visit with them before he went to the beach.

When he pulled up in the driveway, his dad was mowing the grass.

"No wonder I couldn't make contact with you," his dad said, smiling as he reached down to pet Sandy.

"Well, I have been a little busy. Sandy and I had a visit from John Wesley and had him in custody, but he managed to get away."

"That is bad news. I have some Good news for you, but it is nothing to get real excited about."

"What is it?"

"When we got back from the cruise, your mom decided that she wanted someone to help her around the house. We have hired a lady who has been a tremendous help to your mom."

As they entered the house a lady who Jake's dad introduced as May met them.

"May has been helping us out and we have fallen in love with her. She has been helping people in this area for a long time. She has been with us for a couple of weeks and I am loving it because she is also doing some of the things I was helping your mother with."

"Sounds like you are well cared for," Jake said as he entered his mom's office.

"Hello, Jake. We did not know you were coming. Good to see you. You look great."

"I am fine. Sandy and I had a great time in the mountains.

"Can you stay with us for a while?"

"Not really, I need to get to the beach and anyway it looks like I would just be in the way."

"Silly, we would love for you to stay. May is a good cook and your dad is enjoying all the good food and attention. You will stay for lunch won't you?"

"Sure."

"May, include Jake in the lunch plans," she yelled to May, who was passing in the hall.

Yes ma'am, I sure will."

"Dad, I am having a little trouble with one of the tires on my truck. Do you think I can get it taken care of while I am here?"

159

"Sure. Let me call Saul at Cary Car Care."

Jake chatted with his mom while his dad made the phone call.

Coming back into the room, Jake's dad said, "Saul says to bring it over now and they will take care of it."

The two left and met at the repair shop.

"Hello, Jake," Saul said as they entered the shop.

"Long time no see," Jake said as they shook hands.

"Your dad tells me you are enjoying your photography, but are still catching crooks."

"Well, life does stay exciting. Give us a call when you are able to fix my tire."

"Sure will. Good to see you. I was very sorry to hear about Jackie."

"Thanks," Jake said with no other reply as they left the shop.

Lunch included a fresh blueberry pie, which was a favorite of Jake's. After lunch, Jake talked for a while with his mom and dad until the phone rang and Jake's dad said, "They have your truck ready."

"I had better get on the road," Jake said as he went over and kissed his mom.

As they were leaving, Sandy went to the chair and nuzzled Jake's mother as if to say goodbye to her.

"She is such a sweet dog. Sure glad you were able to get her back from that Williams man. I was relieved to know he was back in jail again, but since he escaped I hope they catch him and he stays there this time. He has caused our family enough trouble. Keep in touch. We love you," she said with a tear in her eye as they left the room.

"Jake, do you have time to run by Burke Bros on the way to the garage?"

"Sure, that is still my favorite hardware store in all the world. I just saw an article about them in *Southern Living* magazine."

Jaim and Enry were behind the store counter and Jake stopped to talk to them while Avid took Jake's dad to the specialty screw drawer to find an item he knew he could not find anywhere else in town.

"You fellows amaze me. You have it when no one else does, so that is why I always come here first," he said to Ohnny, who had just walked up.

Jake found some wire and drill bits that he needed for a project and the two men made their purchases and left the store.

After he got his car, Jake and his dad embraced and Mr. Johnson stood in the parking lot and watched Jake pull out of the driveway.

CHAPTER 21

BAD BOY HOUSE BURGLARS

MONDAY, MAY 5, 2003

Back at the beach and on an early morning walk with Sandy, Jake met Susan on the beach and they stopped at the pier for a cup of coffee. Sitting on a fisherman's perch at the end of the pier they caught each other up on what had been happening in their lives. Susan was impressed that Jake had captured John Wesley Williams and was very glad that no harm had come to Sandy. She was also amazed that Williams had been able to escape again.

Susan explained that her job was taking her away from the beach more often to visit other museums and to search for new ideas to incorporate into the Ocean Isle Museum. She told

Jake that she had an alarm system installed in her home because of the increased number of break-ins on the beach. She had bought some new artwork and wanted to protect it.

"Jake, I don't want to impose on you, but you seem very adept at knowing what to do and how to handle the bad guys. Would you consider being on the call list for my alarm system?"

"Well, you know that I come and go, but when I am here I'll be glad to try and help when I can. Sandy and I always look for a little excitement."

"I'll bring some instructions and a key by your place in the next day or two. I'll try to keep you informed by email when I am going to be out of town."

They sat and watched the early morning surfers try to catch a decent wave while the pelicans dove for their food a little farther off shore. Jake caught a whiff of her perfume as the breeze blew his way and decided he should ask her out, but before he could she explained that she had to run so she could get to work. They parted company as they walked off the pier.

Jake silently kicked himself for letting that opportunity go by, but knew that it would be hard to explain to Barbara when she found out he was seeing Susan, even though nothing had been said about them being exclusive. He rationalized that it would have just been a chance to be with a friend and have some supper. He had to admit to himself that he did get lonely and even though Sandy was great company, he still yearned for some female companionship. Susan was beautiful and very easy to be with and did not seem to want anything beyond friendship.

The phone ringing in the middle of the night startled Jake. When he answered, the operator said," Jake Johnson, this is a call from YPC Security System. Dr. Susan McQueen's home system has been compromised and the police are not available. I am notifying you because you are at the top of her call list."

"Thanks, I'll take care of it," Jake said as he shook his head to try to get wide awake.

He turned on the light and got dressed quickly sticking his pistol in his belt as he picked up his keys and a flashlight and headed out the door. He now recalled seeing an email that told him Susan had gone to Columbia, South Carolina for the week.

As he approached Susan's house, he could see lights flashing around inside and down the street a car was parked in an awkward way, not being in a driveway, and as he approached he saw someone duck down so they couldn't be seen as he passed by. He did not stop and did not look at the car. He turned off at the first side street, turned off his lights, and parked his car. He walked back toward the other car keeping in the shadows so he wouldn't be seen. The window on the driver's side was down and Jake put his pistol on the man's neck as he put his hand on the man's shoulder and told him to be quiet and not to move.

"Are your friends in the house armed?" he

asked very harshly.

"No," the young man stuttered.

"Do you have a weapon?" Jake asked.

"No."

"How long have they been in there?" Jake asked.

"They should be coming out very soon."

"What are they after?"

"Drugs and cash."

"Don't try anything foolish because I won't hesitate to shoot you," Jake said very sternly to the man as he opened the door and got in the back seat.

"Who are you?" the boy asked.

"I am former FBI and a friend of the lady who owns the house."

"What are you going to do?"

"We are going to sit here until they come out and you are going to drive up there and pick them up and all four of us are going to the police station. Don't get yourself hurt by trying anything foolish."

In a moment, the two fellows appeared and flashed a light toward the car.

"Let's go," Jake said.

The young man started the car and pulled up beside the two men standing on the sidewalk."

They did not notice Jake until they were in the car.

"Take it easy fellows, I have a gun and will not hesitate to use it. If you run, you will just go to jail tired."

The two stared at Jake and were speechless

as Jake told the driver to go to the police station.

On the way to the station, Jake called 911 and told the operator to have an officer meet him at the Ocean Isle Police Department.

"Well, fellows, did you find anything worth going to jail for?"

"Not really," one of them blurted out. Just a little cash."

Jake saw the cruiser pull into the police station lot just as they passed the motel and turned to go to the police station. Jake directed them to park beside the police car, give him the keys, and sit tight.

"Good morning, Dan. Got three young fellows here who broke into Susan's house looking for cash and drugs."

"Morning, Jake. How did you find them?"

"The security service called me and I was able to get there before they left the house. They might be the ones responsible for some of your other break-in's."

"Let's get them inside and we will see what we have. I don't recognize them.

Jake opened the door and told the three to get out and go into the station. As they entered the building, the chief drove up.

"Jake, what are you up to now."

"These three broke into Susan's house and I thought you might like to talk to them."

"How did you get involved?"

"I am on her call list."

"Why did the deputy not get the call?"

"Sir, I was on a fake 911 call at the other end of the island."

"If you will check their cell phones they probably made the fake 911 call," Jake said. Then he added, "You might check to see if any of the three work for the security company."

"This might clear up some other robberies we have had," the chief added.

"I'll leave the police work to you. I am going back home and try to get some sleep. I'll stop by later and help take care of any paper work needed. Glad I did not have to shoot any of them because I never would have gotten all the paper worked filled out."

"You are right about that. Thanks for your help. Will see you later," the chief said as he slapped Jake on the back on his way out the door.

Jake turned back around and asked, "Chief, can you run me back to Susan's house so I can get my truck? I almost forgot I left it there."

"Sure. Let me tell Dan what is happening and I'll be right with you."

The sky was just beginning to get a little light as Jake waited for the chief. Another beautiful day was in the making. When the chief did not come back in a few minutes Jake decided to go back in to see what was causing the hold up. The chief was on the phone and Jake listened to the one-sided conversation.

"You thought he was staying with friends, but you have checked with all his friends and they do not know where he is."

Pause while the chief listened.

"His bike is missing."

Another pause.

"He said he was going to work on a school project. Mrs. Thompson, I'll be there in a few minutes and we will find Tommy. He couldn't have gone far."

The chief hung up the phone just as Dan entered the room.

"Chief, I have then in a holding cell and have called James to come in and watch the office."

"Tommy Thompson did not come home last night and Mrs. Thompson is beside herself. I am going over to talk to her as soon as I take Jake to pick up his truck. We may need some help in combing the neighborhood, so alert the other deputies that we might need for them to come in."

As they got into the squad car, Jake said, "Chief, why don't I just go with you to the Thomsons'? " I know she is worried sick and maybe I can be of some help."

"Be glad to have your help. We will get your truck later."

"You mind dropping by the house and letting me get Sandy? She is not a professional tracker, but she might be of some help."

Jake bounded up the stairs and in a moment he and Sandy were back. He opened the back door and Sandy hopped right in. They drove off the island and turned left at the stoplight.

They turned into a small development on the waterway and as they approached the house, they could see that a small crowd of neighbors and friends had gathered at the Thompsons'.

The chief spoke to several of the group and found Mr. and Mrs. Thompson, and suggested that they go inside to talk. The chief introduced Jake to the Thompsons and when they entered the house Sandy lay down by the front door.

"Care for some coffee?" Mrs. Thompson asked.

"No, we are fine," Jake and the chief both responded.

"I am going to tan that boy's hide when we find him," Mr. Thompson blurted out.

"When is the last time you saw him?" the chief asked.

"He had been working on a school history project and had been talking to an old fellow over at Gause landing who has been telling him stories about the old days and telling him about George Washington spending the night in the area. He came busting into the house about five o'clock yesterday afternoon and picked up his camera and said he had to go take some pictures and I watched him ride off on his bike. When he did not show up for supper, I thought he had just eaten at a friend's house and forgotten to call. That happens sometimes. After supper, George and I fell asleep in front of the TV and when we woke up we both thought he had come in and gone to bed and we did not think any more about it until we got up to get him off to school and he was not in his room. When we checked with some of his friends and couldn't find anyone that knew where he might be, we called you."

"Mind if I look around in his room a little? Jake asked the Thompsons.

"Not at all. It is just down the hall on the right," Mrs. Thompson said as she went to take the boiling teapot off the stove.

In the room, Jake found some notes about the history project and about William Gause Jr., who was a large landowner back in the 1790's. He had a house at Gause Landing where George Washington had supposedly spent the night and they had breakfast under one of the large live oak trees that lined the road. Jake found an address scribbled on a scrap of paper, together with the name James Knot and 'tomb' in big block letters.

Jake returned to the kitchen where Mrs. Thompson had persuaded the chief to have cup of tea with her.

"I think I know where he might have gone. Is Mr. Knot the person he has been talking to?"

"I think so. He lives over on Gause Landing Road."

"Chief, I think we should go talk to him," Jake said.

"Y'all stay here in case Tommy comes back home. We will be back in touch with you. Tell the folks outside to go back home and we will get in touch with them if we need their help."

The chief and Jake left and went over to Gause Landing Road to try to talk to Mr. Knot. The short winding road was like riding back into the 1700's. Spanish moss drooped down from the live oak trees and the architectural of some of the homes harked back to another century. They find Mr. Knot hoeing weeds in his flower beds.

"Good morning Chief, what brings you over this way?"

"We are looking for Tommy Thompson and understand you have been spending some time with him telling him about the history of this area."

"What has he done? He seems like a nice kid."

"He is not in any trouble. But he did not come home last night and his parents are worried about him."

"I'm Jake Johnson, Mr. Knot. Did you tell Tommy about the Gause tomb off Hale Swamp Road?"

"Yep, I tried to explain to him how to get there and he rode off on his bike saying he was going to try to find it. He was planning to take some pictures and add it to his school report."

Looking at the chief, Jake said, " I know where it is and I bet that is where he has gone."

"Thanks for the information, Mr. Knot," the chief said as he and Jake returned to the car.

"The Historical Society got me to take some pictures of it some time ago so I know right where it is."

"I have heard of it, but have never been there.

Understand it is pretty gown up around it."

"Yeah, the underbrush is pretty thick. There is a small path leading to it that can be difficult to find. It took us a couple of tries when I came to take the pictures."

The chief proceeded past the airport and turned on Hale Swamp Road toward Shallotte and Jake directed him into a small dead end road that ended in the corner of a field where the undergrowth started.

When Jake opened the door, Sandy bounded out and headed toward the underbrush where she stopped and gave one low bark as if to say, come on, you slow pokes. Leaning against a big bush was Tommy's bike.

"Go find him," Jake said to Sandy, patting her on the head.

"Looks like this is where he went," the chief said and radioed Dan that they had found the bike.

Sandy led them down a very small path that was difficult for the men to get through, but in a few minutes they saw the brick structure that Jake was looking for.

"Tommy," Jake yelled at the top of his voice.

They heard a muffled reply of, "Help!" but they could not see anyone. Sandy went to the brick structure and gave a loud bark. The chief and Jake went in that direction and found an opening.

The chief yelled, "Tommy, are you in there? Are you all right?"   "Yeah. I am all right, but I am hungry and tired. I did not get much sleep last night. I came in through that hole, but was not able to get out. I have been here all night and I was scared!"

"We will get you out," Jake said as he lay down on the ground and reached into the hole.

"Can you reach my arms?"

"Not quite," Tommy yelled back.

"I have a chain ladder in the back of the patrol car. I'll get it," the chief said as he left to return to the car.

"Anything down there?" Jake asked Tommy.

"Nothing I can see. It is pretty dark down here and I was glad I couldn't see anything. I was afraid there might be snakes or big spiders. I was leaning into the hole trying to get some pictures when my camera slipped out of my hand, and when I tried to reach it I slipped into the hole. I used my camera flash to see that there was nothing down here, no snakes or dead bodies. I used the flash so much I ran the batteries down. Can you get me out?"

"Yes, the chief is coming with a ladder that will let you climb out. Your parents are going to be glad you are all right. This should make a nice report for your school project. No other kids will have had an experience like this."

The chief returned with the ladder and they lowered it into the tomb and Tommy climbed out with a big smile on his face.

"Let's get you home to your parents," the chief said, putting his arm around Tommy's shoulders as they walked back to the car.

They put Tommy's bike in the back of the car

and he and Sandy got into the back seat. Sandy laid her head in his lap and he stroked her head as they took Tommy back to his home. His mom and dad were waiting in the yard when they arrived. Tommy bounded out of the car and gave his mom and dad a big hug and then told them he was hungry.

The parents thanked the chief and Jake, and took Tommy into the house as he chattered away about what had happened to him.

"Come on, Jake I'll take you to pick up your truck. Thanks for your and Sandy's help. I am glad it had a happy ending."

CHAPTER 22

MODERN DAY PIRATES

TUESDAY, MAY 13, 2003

Jake was sitting on his porch absorbed in reading the Christian Science Bible Lesson when he heard a car pull into his driveway and someone run up the stairs and knock on his door. Sandy stood up and looked through the picture window at the street side door wagging her tail, so Jake knew that it was someone she knew. When he reached the door he was pleasantly surprised to see Susan.

"Good morning," she said as she opened the storm door and came in. "Excuse me for busting in on you, but I have a favor to ask."

"No problem, how can I help?"

"I know that you do not gamble or drink, but I have some visitors coming in to see the museum and they want to take one of the gambling cruises out of Little River and I would love to have some company since I am not interested in the gambling or drinking. Thought we might enjoy a good meal and just hang out while they do their thing. You might have to help me get them back to the motel if they have a bad night. I don't know these people very well and I sure would love to have your company."

"When are you talking about? Might have a hard time fitting it into my busy schedule," Jake said, laughing.

"We will need to leave Ocean Isle about 4 p.m. on Friday evening. The cruise lasts about five hours. I'll pick up the tab if you will just go with me and rescue me from a very dull evening with people I do not know all that well."

"Well, I think I can handle that if you promise that you will not get drunk on me," Jake said, smiling as Susan punched him in the stomach teasingly.

"Have to run. Will call you about the details later," she said as she stooped down to pet Sandy, who had placed herself between Susan and the door and was not going to let her out without at least one pat on the head.

Jake watched as she went down the stairs and waved to her as she drove off.

"Well Sandy, she looks better every time I see her. What are we going to do when she and Barbara finally surface together?"

Sandy looked up at him with what appeared to

be a smile on her face that said, you got yourself into this and you will have to get yourself out.

When Friday rolled around, Jake took Sandy down to the pier, where Calvin said he would be glad to look after her while Jake was gone.

Promptly at four, Susan pulled up in the museum van and introduced Jake to the visitors.

"Jake Johnson, this is Peter O'toole and his wife Mary from Hershey, Pennsylvania, and Jackie and Jeff Peterson from York, Pennsylvania. They have been touring our museum and are ready for a little fun and excitement tonight."

"Good to meet you all and welcome to the great state of North Carolina. Susan, would you like for me to drive?"

"No. Not now, maybe on the way home."

Jake engaged the four in conversation as Susan concentrated on getting them to the dock on time.

When they arrived at the waterfront, they were all excited to see the Big M Gambling Boat at the dock with all the people being ushered aboard.

As the sun began to set, the boat moved down the river into Little River Inlet and out into the ocean. The patrons lined the deck and watched as the beautiful scenery slowly went by. They stared in wonder at the serene wildlife scenes and the beautiful golf courses. The water was calm and the breeze was pleasant as they moved out of the inlet into the ocean. The boat crew began to offer cocktails and to steer people into the dining room for entertainment until they could reach International waters where gambling would be allowed.

Susan was the perfect host as Jake stood back and admired her beauty and comfortable way with people. The buffet left nothing to be desired and they all ate too much and some of the patrons began to drink too much also. The crew knew that plying the people with alcohol would make the money flow easier.

When the gambling started Jake, and Susan retired to the fantail of the boat where they could sit and talk. The night was beautiful with moonlight sparkling on the water. They found a little niche where they were out of the wind and were enjoying their privacy when Jake noticed two fast boats in the distance overtaking the Big M.

The boats split and went to either side of the boat. Men with guns boarded the boat and rushed up the stairs to the wheelhouse while others stationed themselves around on the deck and at the entrances to the lower decks. One quick blast from a machine gun got everyone's attention and after the yelling stopped, one of the gang shouted, "This is not a game. Everyone cooperate and no one will get hurt. We are here for your money and your valuables. Fill our bags and we will be on our way and no one will get hurt."

They went among the passengers and crew collecting money, jewelry, cell phones, etc. as people gasped and cried.

Jake and Susan were out of sight and Susan looked at Jake and asked, "What should we do?"

"I am not sure, but you stay here and let me go see what I can do," he said as he instinctively reached for his gun which he usually carried in the small of his back, but tonight he had left at home.

"Do you have your cell phone?"

"Yes."

"Stay hidden, but if any of them come back out on deck engage them in conversation to distract them from what I am doing. Get in touch with the Coast Guard and tell them what is happening. I'll see what I can do with their boats."

Jake slowly moved in the direction of the tied up boat on the starboard side of the gambling boat. In the boat were four sets of scuba gear. Jake opened the valves on each tank to let most of the oxygen out. He then cut a hole in the engine's fuel line. When he was finished in that boat, he moved carefully to the port side and did the same thing with that boat. Going back to where Susan was still hidden, he asked her," Did you get the Coast Guard?"

"Yes."

By this time the men began emerging from the interior of the boat carrying two sacks of money and other valuables and headed for their boats. When those six were in the boats, the two others emerged from the wheelhouse and joined them. Jake heard the motors start up and watched as they moved away from the boat. He rushed up the stairs to the wheelhouse and told the captain, "Move your vessel away from those boats. They are going to be dead in the water in a few minutes, but we need to be out of gunshot range. The Coast Guard is on its way."

"They disabled our radio. How did you get in touch with the Coast Guard?"

"My friend used her cell phone. We were on the fantail of the ship and they never did see us. I cut their gas lines and disabled their scuba gear. They should be easy to pick up later."

"Who are you?"

"I am Jake Johnson, a former FBI agent who was having a nice evening on your ship with my friend Susan."

"Go take care of the passengers and we will help with the Coast Guard when they arrive. Keep the passengers below deck until we get this resolved."

Watching the two boats with binoculars Jake saw one sputter to a stop and in a few minutes the other one did the same. The men hastened to put on their scuba gear, but quickly realized that their tanks were almost empty and threw the gear into the bottom of the boat.

Jake and Susan heard the helicopter approaching and not far behind was the Coast Guard cruiser which pulled up beside the boat. Jake yelled at them that the men were stranded in their boats about two hundred yards off the port bow. The cruiser and helicopter left. Jake watched through binoculars as they encountered the men in the boat who raised their hands and did not give any resistance.

The cruiser returned to the gambling boat and

tied up alongside. The Coast Guard returned the two bags of valuables to the captain. They took statements from the captain and crew, and from some of the passengers and Jake.

The Coast Guard Captain, Royce Garrett, thanked Jake for his help and told him his quick thinking had averted the robbery. He relayed that this had happened on other ships in other ports. The crooks would leave the target ship and all but the drivers of the boats would go to shore with their scuba gear and there was no way to trace them and no evidence to hold the drivers.

On the way back to Ocean Isle, Susan's guest were excited and chattered about their adventure all the way home. After depositing the folks at the motel, Jake drove back to his place and invited Susan in. She said she was exhausted from all the excitement and had better get home because she had to be at work early the nest morning.

"Give me a rain check. I would love to, but I wouldn't be too much fun tonight."

She gave Jake a kiss on the cheek and a hug and thanked him for all he had done. The whiff of her perfume brought back memories to Jake of their night on the beach working with the sea turtles. As she left, he said, "I'll call you to collect on my rain check."

CHAPTER 23

SMOKY MOUNTAIN ELK

TUESDAY, MAY 27, 2003

Jake was ready for his next photography assignment. He had had enough of the cloak and dagger stuff. He was ready for some peace and quiet in the deep woods of the Great Smoky Mountain National Park. The Park Service had hired him to do a photographic study of the elk that had been introduced back into North Carolina and Tennessee in 2001 when they imported 25 animals into the park and added another 27 in 2003. He was going to spend some time camping and following the elk herd that had now grown to about 60.

He had asked Barbara to go with him and she was thrilled at the idea, but had to decline when her work took her to California to work on several pending cases in that area. He was going to have to be content with having Sandy for company. The rangers had given him special permission to take her with him. Normally dogs were not allowed to roam without a leash in the national park, but Jake had convinced them that she wouldn't cause any trouble and that he needed some company.

He had left his beach house under the careful supervision of Hazel Simpson and hoped that she would be able to rent it for the time he would be away. He had said his good-byes to Susan without having collected on her rain check, but hoped that would happen as soon as he returned from this assignment.

He and Sandy drove to Asheville and spent the night in his cabin before leaving for the national park. He wanted to check in with Ken before he left.

"Hello, Ken, this is Jake,"

"Hello, buddy. Where are you?"

"I'm at the cabin getting ready to head out to the Great Smokies in the morning with Sandy to do a photo shoot of the elk."

"Yeah I heard about that. Barbara told me she was not going to be able to go and that Sandy was going with you."

"When did you talk to her?"

"She called about some more of the details about John Wesley Williams, but I think she just wanted to say hello. How long are you going to be gone?"

"Not sure. Depends on how we get along

tracking the elk. Probably two or three weeks. I need to get away so I might stretch it out for a while. It is a contract price and they don't care how long it takes."

"Sounds like fun. I would invite myself along, but it is vacation time here and we are a little short-handed."

"Would appreciate it if you would have someone drop by the cabin every now and then just to see that it is OK."

"Sure, Sam lives out that way and it is no trouble for him to check on it for you."

"Never know when John Wesley or one of his henchmen will try to come back. I do have the alarm system set to call your office if someone actually gets into the house again."

"We will keep it safe for you. Have a good trip and we will see you when you get back."

The call of the whipporwill and the rushing sound of Reams Creek was music to Jake's ears and Sandy seemed to be content to be back in the mountains again also.

Jake had packed the night before and at 5:30 in the morning was wide awake and ready to leave on his new adventure. Sandy was right at his heels and was sure she was not going to be left behind. At 6:15 they were in the truck heading for Highway 40 and later connected with Highway 19 into Bryson City. They stopped for their last store-bought meal and even though Sandy had to stay in the truck and wait for hers, she seemed happy to just be there with Jake.

Jake enjoyed the drive up to the Deep Creek Ranger Station and wished he had time to do a little fishing, but maybe that would come later in the trip.

Ron, the Ranger Jake had met on his last trip into the Smokies, was there waiting for him.

"Hello Jake, it's good to see you again."

"I'm glad to be back up here. This is Sandy. Appreciate your letting me take her with me."

"I know you will be glad for the company. It can get lonely if you are going to be up in the high country for a while. We have your horse and pack mule all ready to go. The horse is Big Red and the mule is Mabel. They are real veterans and have made the trip to the fire tower many times. They probably could go by themselves if we just pointed them in the right direction. We have already packed in some feed and hay up by the fire tower. If you do not use it all, it will keep until fire season starts. Believe you will enjoy the animals more than the ATV you used last time. They will be quieter and give you a better chance to see the wildlife. As we discussed, you can make the fire tower your base camp and take side trips out from there. There is a corral where you can leave the animals. We have electric fences in place to keep the bears out. Leave them some water and feed and they would be good for a couple of days."

"It has been a while since I have been on a horse, but I am sure it will come back quickly. I had several years' experience at Philmont Scout Ranch working with pack animals. It sure will beat lugging all this equipment up the mountain on my back and the horse will give me a chance to cover a lot more ground in tracking the elk."

"You should be able to make the fire tower by late afternoon. Be sure to check in with us from time to time. We have had some problems with poachers. I am sure you have your sidearm, but we have also included a 30.30 rifle just in case you might need it. There are extra cartridges in the saddle bag."

"What have the poachers been after?"

"They are not too particular. Deer, elk or bear, whatever they come across. If you see any signs let us know and we will send a team in."

"Well, I've had all the contact I want with the bad guys lately so I'll leave that part up to you. Reckon we had better get going."

Jake and Ron secured Jake's personal items on the packsaddle with a diamond hitch and Jake checked the cinch on the pack mule and on Big Red.

"You fellows were great to take care of all the food and gear. I really appreciate that."

"You will find the menu in with the food list and if we have forgotten anything let us know. Someone usually makes the rounds to the fire tower every so often to check on campers and hikers in the area, so we can bring in what you might need."

After saying his goodbye's, Jake mounted Big Red and Ron watched as he led Mabel up the trail with Sandy trotting along beside them. This is great. Getting paid to do something I love to do in this beautiful setting is unbelievable, Jake thought. The billowing white clouds, the beautiful blue sky, and the dark green of the forest cover made a beautiful picture and Jake was enjoying every minute of it.

Sandy ran ahead to the first fording of Deep Creek. She stopped for a drink of the cool, clear water and Big Red and Mabel also stopped and took a drink. As Jake sat in the saddle in the middle of the stream, he picked out several spots where he would have dropped his fly if he had had time to fish, but he wanted to be sure to make the fire tower by sundown.

This was repeated several times as the trail meandered back and forth across Deep Creek and then took a more direct route to the crest of the mountains where Jake followed the trail to the fire tower. He was now back into somewhat familiar territory as he had spent several weeks up here doing his photo shoot on the wolves.

He was glad the long ride was over and it took him a minute to get his walking legs back under him. It had been a long time since he had ridden that far on a horse. He unsaddled Big Red and put him in the corral and then unpacked the packsaddle and stored all the gear in the cabin. Later he would brush and curry both of the animals, but now he needed to get things set up for his stay in the mountains. Sandy made a tour of the facilities and came back with her approval, and followed Jake around as he finished up his chores.

He built a fire in the little stove to take the chill off the cabin and to heat some water for a later shower. He checked in with Ron at the ranger station to let him know that he was safe and sound on top of the mountain. He felt like he was on top of the world as he looked out over the beautiful mountains with Tennessee on one side and North Carolina on the other. Shortly after dark he was ready for bed and the canvas bunk felt like a featherbed as he quickly drifted off to sleep to the night sounds of the high mountains.

The bright sun flooded the room and Jake was wide-awake. He had had a very good night and as he lay in the bunk he remembered the storm on his last trip the night before he found the case with the money. That whole adventure and the hectic days that followed seemed like a dream, but it had turned out well in the end and now he had Barbara in his life. He so wished that she had been able to come with him on this trip.

His plan for the day was to hike to the high meadow in search of the elk herd and if need be he would spend the night there, so he prepared his pack accordingly. He curried Big Red and Mabel and left them water and feed and off he went with Sandy at his side.

He was very pleased as he approached the meadow because he could see six elk grazing along one edge. With his camera in hand he carefully moved into a position where they wouldn't pick up his scent as he got closer for some better shots.

Moving from tree to tree along the edge of the meadow, he got within fifty yards of them before he sensed that they were getting a little edgy. He stopped and lay on the ground watching without making a move. Every now and then they would give a glance in his direction and as soon as he could, he would take some more pictures. Eventually they started moving back into the woods and when they were out of sight he started following them and could see the trails they used to come and go from the meadow. He wanted to try to determine their patterns so he could situate himself in a position to get some closer shots of individual elk as well as of the whole herd. He had yet to see one of the big bulls.

When their trail crossed a little creek, he went upstream for a little way and decided to make camp for the night. He would stay there to see if they used this trail daily to go back and forth to the meadow. It was shielded from the trail so they couldn't see him. He built a small fire and he and Sandy had their supper and he was ready to try to get some sleep. It had been a while since he had hiked that much in one day. As he lay in his bedroll with Sandy at his feet, he enjoyed the night sounds of the deep woods. He drifted off to sleep, but was awakened by the howl of a wolf in the distance. He thought that it probably was one of the wolves he had photographed on his last trip to the Smokies.

He also heard the trumpeting of what sounded like a big bull elk, but the more he listened, he determined it was someone trying to call the elk. It was not hunting season and the warning the ranger had given him about poachers came to mind. He lay there listening to the night creatures and trying to get back to sleep when he heard a shot. Sandy's head perked up and Jake sat upright in his bedroll. Darn those fellows he thought. Why do they have to disturb this wonderful wilderness and hurt these beautiful animals?

There were no more shots so he lay back down and adjusted his pillow and in a few minutes was back to sleep.

The sunlight filtering through the large trees was beautiful as he lay there thinking about what the day might bring. Sandy's head perked up and she stared toward the trail. Jake put his hand on her head and patted her and whispered to her to be still. He then heard the elk herd passing by on their way to the meadow. He put on his boots, grabbed his camera, snapped a leash on Sandy, and then made his way toward the trail. He was able to get close enough to get some good shots. This time there was a big bull with them and he was surrounded by his harem. Jake stayed parallel to their trail and made it to the edge of the meadow, where he had a perfect view of them as they grazed in the beautiful sunlit field. It was still early enough that the sun had not burned off the haze and it looked like a fairyland with these beautiful large animals grazing on the lush green grass. After watching them for about an hour, he returned to his camp to a happy tail-wagging dog.

They ate and Jake decided he would backtrack on the trail to try to find where they bedded down for the night. When he was well away from the meadow he decided he would call Ron on the radio and report the gunshot he had heard during the night. Evidently he was in an area where the radio wouldn't work and he put it away, thinking that he would try again later. He kept talking to Sandy about how beautiful this was and Sandy looked at him as if to acknowledge that she knew exactly what he was saying.

After a couple of miles on this trail, he began to see horse tracks as well as elk tracks. He could make out three different sets of tracks. When they left the elk trail, he decided to follow the horse trail. After another mile he found a deserted campsite that looked like it had been used recently. From the layout of the camp he determined that there were two people and their horses, plus a pack animal. Near the campsite he found the carcass of a bull elk. The antlers had been removed and the body butchered to take out some of the prized meat pieces. Jake documented his find with a lot of detailed photographs. He tried again to contact Ron, but the radio still would not go through.

Looking closer at the carcass he found poison pellets scattered on the body, probably to kill the wolves that would eventually find the body and devour it. He put Sandy back on her leash so she wouldn't get into the pellets and then began to clean up the carcass. He buried the pellets and piled rocks on top so that no animal would get into them.

191

These rascals have to be stopped, Jake thought. I wonder how often they come in here to do this kind of thing?

Jake took more pictures of the campsite and the carcass and decided to head back to the fire tower. When he got back to the meadow he could see the herd lying under some trees on the far side. He made a wide berth because he did not want to spook them. In mid-afternoon when he reached the fire tower, he tried to reach Ron again. but the radio was not working.

I'll have to take care of this on my own he thought. I am not going to let them get away with this. In the cabin he found a map of the area and determined where the poachers might be entering the park.

He began devising a plan on how to catch them in the act and take them to the authorities. He did not know how far these poachers would go to protect themselves from being taken to jail.

He fixed a quick supper, ate in haste, and saddled Big Red. He put his rifle in the scabbard on the saddle and put on a holster with his handgun. Strapped his bedroll to the back of the saddle and put a couple of cans of beanie weenies in the saddle bags along with some bottled water and a pouch of dog food for Sandy. He tried the radio again, but was unable to make contact with anyone.

Dusk was settling in as he left the fire tower, but the sky was clear and he knew that there would be a full moon and he would have plenty of light to follow the trail. It was a pleasant ride and Sandy trotted along right in front of Big Red like she was leading the way.

He stopped on the edge of the bald and watched for any movement along the tree line and in the grassland. By the light of the moon he could see the herd moving on to the grass and beginning to graze. He picked his way around the edge of the big meadow to get to the trail he had been on earlier. He did not want to spook the herd nor did he want the poachers to see him. A lone wolf howl cut through the night air and made Big Red shiver, but Jake patted her on the neck and talked softly to her and she calmed sown very quickly. Sandy's ears perked up, but with a word from Jake she too settled down.

Jake dismounted and watched as the herd came to attention and stopped grazing, and grew very intent on being on guard. After a few moments of silence the herd began to graze again. Jake caught a reflection from something at the edge of the forest. With his binoculars he could see two men sitting on horseback at the edge of the clearing. The herd had not moved into their range of sight and Jake wanted to get to them before they were able to kill any more of the animals. He tethered Big Red to a tree and he and Sandy moved back into the forest and started working their way toward the two men. They were about one hundred feet apart and had gotten off their horses and were intent on watching for the herd unaware of Jake and Sandy approaching them from the rear. The wet moss underfoot let Jake move in very close without being detected. When he was near the first man, he said in a very soft, but firm voice, "Be quiet and put your gun down."

He turned around very quickly, but when he saw the rifle staring him in the face he put his gun down and said, "Who the hell are you?"

"I am Jake Johnson and if you want to get off this mountain alive you had better do as I say. Put your hands against that tree and stand still. Jake put his riffle against the man's back as he frisked him. He did not find another gun, but took the hunting knife from the man's sheaf and threw it over by the gun.

"Lay face down on the ground and don't move. I know your friend is just over that little ridge and I want you to call him over here. If you cooperate neither one of you will get hurt, but if you try anything stupid I will shoot you right where you lie and my friend will shoot your partner. I know that you have been poaching."

"Take it easy mister. Are you the law?"

"I am as far as you are concerned because you are going to jail if you live. Now, what is your name?"

"Luke."

"What is your friend's name?"

"Joe."

"Well, Luke, call Joe over here and let's get on with it."

He whistled and said, "Joe. Come here."

When the man approached, Jake stepped out from behind the tree and said very firmly, "Put down the gun right now."

The man raised his rifle, but when he saw Jake's rifle pointing straight at him he lowered his rifle and put it on the ground.

"Step away from the gun and put your hands against the tree."

Jake searched him and finding no gun, he told the man to lie down on the ground.

"Is there anyone else with you?" Jake asked.

"No," both men blurted out.

"Well, if there is you may rest assured that the two of you will be my first targets. I am going to take you to the authorities and you can make it easy or hard. If you try to take advantage of me in any way I will shoot you on the spot and not think anything about it. I am a former FBI agent and will not put my life in danger. Do you understand me?"

"Yes," they both answered.

"Sandy here will not bother you unless you try to get up, so please do not try anything. I do not want to have to patch you up before I take you in to the authorities."

Sandy would probably just lick their faces, but they did not know that.

"Where are your horses?"

"They are back down the trail about one half mile."

"Is the pack animal there also?"

"Yes."

"Where did you park your truck and trailer?"

"It is on a service road at the edge of the park."

"Well, we are going to gather up your stuff and go to your truck where I will have the authorities waiting for us. Now slowly get on your feet and don't give Sandy any reason to attack you or me to shoot you."

Jake kept them in front of him with Sandy at his side as he went to where he had tied big Red. He took a rope from his saddle and tied one end around Luke. About ten feet back he tied it around Joe's waist and put the end around his saddle horn. With two shorter pieces of rope he tied each man's hands together in front of him. He put his rifle back in the scabbard, unsnapped the strap on his revolver, and told the men to head out.

The bright moonlit sky made it easy to follow the trail. When they reached the camp, Jake told them to pack up their stuff and to mount their horses. He put the packhorse on a tether behind him and they began their trip back to the service road with the two men still roped together.

Jake made radio contact with a ranger station and got patched through to Ron at the Deep Creek Station and explained what had happened. They agreed on a time that Ron would have rangers meet Jake and take the prisoners into custody.

The trip down the mountain went without a hitch and when they arrived at the trucks, the sun was just lighting up the sky and there were two rangers waiting for them.

"Fellows, I am Jake Johnson and this is Luke and Joe. They've been bad boys and have been poaching on federal land. I have photos to prove it."

"I'm Willis and this is Suzy and we are familiar with these two. We have been trying to get some evidence on them and glad that you were able to do that. Ron tells us you are up here taking some pictures of the elk herd."

"Yeah. I still have some more to do and would have been through with this area if these two had not interfered. Sandy and I are going to head back up to the fire tower and finish our assignment. I will give Ron the information I have when I see him in a few days."

Jake mounted Big Red and headed back up the trail. Jake was so tired he let the reins drop and took a little nap, but big Red just headed back to the fire tower.

Right before they come out onto the big meadow, Jake was awakened and had enough time to move off the trail as the elk herd began to move off the meadow back into the deep woods to spend the day in the shade. He was in a perfect position to take a lot of photographs of the entire herd. After they were gone, he started back to the fire tower.

At the fire tower, Jake fed the two horses and Sandy and lay down across the bunk. When he awakened, the sun was just going down. He fixed himself some supper, took a shower, and then crawled back into the bunk.

Sandy woke him up just as the sun was coming up and let him know that she was ready to go outside. Jake lay back down and went over in his mind all the photos he had taken and decided he had enough for what the Park Service was interested in.

After breakfast he packed up and secured the buildings and headed back down the mountain. The air was crisp and cool and Jake felt good about his pictures and about having captured the two poachers. He wondered what might be in store for him next. John Wesley was still a thorn in his side as they had not been able to find him yet. Maybe something had happened while he was away. If he had not been out of cell phone range, he would have loved to have talked to Barbara and to have caught up with Susan.

He recalled the last time he had made the trip down from the fire tower. He had been very upset about the information he had found in the briefcase. Now most of that had been resolved and his life was back on an even keel.

By mid-afternoon he had arrived at the Deep Creek Ranger Station and had unpacked his packhorse and stowed his gear in his truck. As he was finishing up, Ron, the District Ranger, came out to talk to him about his trip. Ron had already been informed about the capture of the poachers and was very pleased. They talked a little while about the exchange of information Ron Asked if Jake would be available to appear and Jake said he certainly would be there. He wanted to do whatever was necessary to see that those two paid for their slaughter of the animals and the attempted poisoning of the wolves.

Jake shook Ron's hand and he headed back to his mountain cabin. This time he was a little sad that he would not be returning to see Barbara. Sandy must have felt his loneliness because she rode a long way with her head in his lap before she decided she wanted the wind blowing in her face.

On the way home, Jake began to talk to Sandy about how he had to prepare for a return visit from John Wesley Williams. He knew that it was just a matter of time before he would be around, trying to get his money back or taking his anger out on Jake's hide. His mountain cabin was pretty secure and he felt safe when he was there. The beach cottage was more public, but did not provide much protection if John Wesley wanted to make an unannounced visit. Sandy acted interested, but she was ready for some peace and quiet and decided she would rather have the wind blowing in her face on the rest of the trip back to Buncombe County.

CHAPTER 24

BEACH HOUSE PREPARATIONS

MONDAY, JUNE 2, 2003

Jake spent a few days at the cabin enjoying the things he had missed while in the Smokies. What he missed most was some human companionship, and coming back to the cabin from the mountains without Barbara being there to greet him was a real letdown. He talked to her on the phone and checked in with Ken to see if there was any news about John Wesley.

The vulnerability of the beach house played on his mind because he wanted to spend a lot more time there, but he also wanted to be safe. After a few days, he packed up and he and Sandy hit the road south out of the mountains and headed toward the white sandy beaches.

The first thing he decided to do was to put

some film on the windows so he could see out, but no one could see in. He put it only on the windows where someone could see in from outside. He did not cover the windows that were not over the decks.

A trip to Radio Shack provided all the materials he needed for an alarm system and a surveillance system. He set up the alarm system with different sounds to indicate when different areas were breached. It included the driveway and all the perimeters of the house. The accessible windows and doors were set to send a signal to the police station if they were broken or opened when the system was in operation.

The next thing he needed to do was to devise a method of getting out of the house without using the front or back door. He made a trip to Lowe's, bought some material, and began working on his plan. He placed all the material in the storeroom so no one would be able to tell that he was doing any work. He partitioned off his under-house storage unit by putting a false wall inside that formed a small room that was not noticeable upon entering the storage unit, He fixed a door that was not visible from the outside, but looked like part of the outdoor shower stall, that would let him get out of the cottage through the outdoor shower stall.

Next he fixed a trap door that was inside a closet in his bedroom and could be easily opened and closed without being detected. He built a small stairway that let him go downstairs to the storage unit. His main concern was to make it so that Sandy could also use it. He had thought about a fireman's pole which would have allowed for a quick and noiseless escape, but was impracticable because Sandy would have been stuck in the house and John Wesley would like to have another crack at her.

He wired his little hideaway with electricity and placed hidden cameras in each upstairs room, with the monitors in his little hideaway. One switch activated all the cameras, including some covering the decks and under the house. He checked for light leaks and insulated the little room for sound. He worked to get all the creaks out of the stairs and to make sure the trap door was invisible when shut. He stocked the room with some non-perishable food and water for both him and Sandy. He placed a 410 shotgun and a pistol upstairs and downstairs. When he was finished after three days, he was pleased with his work and it had passed all his tests.

Now he could relax a little and enjoy the sun and sounds of the beach. Sandy could not get enough of playing in the surf and she was the talk of the beach as she chased sticks and balls while getting pounded by the surf, but kept coming back and asking for more.

Jake was glad that Susan was out of town for a few days while he had finished his project. He did not really want anyone to know about it.

CHAPTER 25

FLIGHT OF THE WOODPECKER

MONDAY, JUNE 3, 2003

Jake got an urgent call from the Wildlife Commission seeking his help. Some hunter had reported seeing a very large woodpecker in the Big Swamp area in lower Robeson County. They wanted Jake to go into the area to try to get some photographs to determine which woodpecker it might be, hoping that it might be the Ivory-billed Woodpecker that everyone thought was extinct. They wanted him to go immediately and that was fine with Jake because he had finished his project at the beach house and was getting a little restless.

He agreed to get his equipment together and to start out first thing in the morning. It was no real chore as everything was still pretty much intact from his trip to the Smokies. He just needed to repack it in some watertight containers in case of a boat mishap on the river or in the swamp. He replaced his tent with a jungle hammock that would keep him off the wet ground and away from any snakes and mosquitoes.

After checking in with Chief Prevatte and asking that they keep an eye on his place in case John Wesley showed up, Jake was finished with all the things he needed to do. He decided to leave the beach in the late afternoon, pick up a canoe from the Forest Service office, and spend the night in a motel near Lumberton. It took several phone calls to find a motel that was pet friendly, but all the arrangements were made quickly and by four o'clock he and Sandy were off on their new adventure.

After checking into the motel, he and Sandy went to the Brown Derby Drive-In to get some supper. The place was just as he had remembered it. It still had the unpaved parking lot with the curb boys running around taking orders and delivering food. The hamburger and shake were as good as he remembered them and Sandy gulped down the simple hamburger and fries Jake had ordered for her.

They went on a quick drive around town to bring back old memories and then Jake and Sandy were back at the motel because he wanted to get an early start in the morning. After Jake's shower he took Sandy for a quick walk to get her settled for the night and then he was off to bed without even turning on the TV. He knew if he got started he would end up staying up too late.

After picking up a quick breakfast from Bojangles he headed for the Princess Ann Landing boat ramp where he put in his canoe and secured all his gear in case of a mishap. He fastened his camera with a lanyard that would allow him to use it, but would also keep it from ending up at the bottom of the river in case something happened. He had his pistol in case he needed to take care of any snakes.

The mist on the river made for an eerie feeling, but it was like going home to Jake, who had spent a lot of his boyhood on this river. Sandy took her place in the front of the boat and Jake shoved off and headed up river to find the place where Big Swamp emptied into the river.

The canoe cut silently through the water and several ducks took flight as Jake rounded one of the many bends in the river. The water level was at a good stage and paddling upstream was not that hard. Within an hour, Jake was at the point where the swamp water joined the river. This was actually new territory for him, but he was excited to be there. As the sun cut the mist off the river and swamp, he enjoyed hearing the songs of the many birds also beginning their day. He was familiar with a lot of the birdcalls, but strained his ears to try to hear anything that would give him a clue about his prey, the large woodpecker. He heard the rat at tat of some smaller species, but nothing that sounded the alarm in his head. The channel was pretty deep and made for easy paddling as Jake made his way deeper and deeper into the swamp. The Forest Service had provided a map and had pointed out the general area where the hunters had seen the woodpecker. Jake noticed several tributaries feeding into the main swamp race, but was able to continue farther and farther into the swamp without any real difficulties. He had to lift his canoe over a couple of downed logs, but they were so slippery from the moss and water that it was very easy to get over them. As he rounded a bend, he caught sight of a couple of otters playing on the slick, muddy bank. He got a couple of quick pictures before they scurried off into a hiding place until he had passed.

The sun was getting higher and the mist had all burned off, uncovering a beautiful blue sky with a little breeze that made for a very comfortable day. The insect repellent seemed to be working both for him and Sandy, and Jake was enjoying himself immensely. It was hard to believe that a person could get paid for doing what he loved to do. He had a twinge of sadness as he thought about how much his deceased wife, Jackie, would have loved to have been with him. He thought that Barbara would really like it also, but there had not been time to invite her on this trip. He would just have to be content with Sandy on this trip, which was all right with him.

Jake was brought back to reality as he rounded a bend in the river and met an old man paddling a dugout canoe. His cane fishing pole was hanging out over the bow and his shotgun was by his side.

Jake threw up his hand and said, "Good morning. Do you have a minute? I would like to talk to you for a moment."

The old man pulled his dugout canoe along side Jake's canoe and grasped the gunnel so that they floated along together.

"Nice looking dog you have there," the old man said as Sandy shifted her position and licked him on the hand.

"That's Sandy and she is harmless as a kitten. I'm Jake Johnson and am looking to try to take some pictures of some big woodpeckers."

"I'm Nash Odom and I just been up the swamp fishing all night."

"I see from your stringer that you have not just been fishing, but you have been catching also."

The old man smiled as he lifted the stringer out of the water to reveal a very nice mess of fish.

"Yep, they were biting pretty good. What kind of woodpeckers are you looking for?"

"There is a big one with a long bill called an Ivory-billed Woodpecker that was thought to be all gone, but some hunters reported seeing one in these parts. Have you seen any unusual-looking birds on your trips up here?"

"Back in the spring when the leaves were just coming out, I caught a glimpse of a large black and white bird with a red crest, but the leaves were so thick I could not get a good look at him. I heard a lot of 'rat-tat-tat', but I never saw him again. I have seen some trees with large rectangular holes that looked like some big bird must have been trying to dig out the grubs and ants and other insects."

"There are two different birds that are very similar, but the Ivory-billed is larger than the Pileated. Do you remember where that might have been?"

"It was about a mile and half up the creek, at one of my favorite fishing spots. If you just keep going upstream you will come to two big cypress trees on the right hand side in the curve of the swamp where I have tied a white rag on the lower limb to mark my spot. It was in that area that I saw the big bird."

"I need to spend several days up here. Is there any high ground where I might make camp?"

"If you go east out of the main channel and out through the swamp, you will come to a small thicket of pines that would be a nice, dry place to camp. Old man Simpson use to have a still up there before he passed away several years ago. The sheriff busted up his last still, but there might still be some of it still lying around. There is a good fresh water spring there where the water is safe to drink. It made some pretty good white lightning in its day."

"That sounds like it will be a good place to camp. Will you be coming back up this way any time soon?"

"Probably not. Going deer hunting with some fellows over in Bladen County. You and Sandy take care and be careful of the snakes. There are a lot out this year. I best be going, my old lady will be wondering what has happened to me. I promised her I would be home pretty early this morning."

Jake shook the old man's hand and thanked him for all his good information.

"Hope you get a good big buck," Jake said as he watched the dugout canoe glide peacefully away. In a minute it was out of sight around a bend in the run of the swamp.

Jake steered the canoe back into the main channel and with long easy strokes he had the canoe moving quickly upstream through the slow-moving water.

Sandy settled back into position as lookout in the boat and Jake enjoyed the sounds of the swamp as it came alive in the early morning hours.

By noon he had reached the two big cypress tress with the white rag. He maneuvered the canoe where he could tie it up to a cypress knee and decided to try some fishing. He got out his fly rod and tied on a popping bug and a trailing black ant. His first cast, which he bounced off one of the big cypress trees, resulted in a flurry of activity as a big blue gill hit the popper as soon as it hit the water. In a moment Jake boated the fish and Sandy perked up as the fish flopped around in the bottom of the boat. With a word from Jake, Sandy settled down. He certainly did not need her overturning the boat. He was not interested in a cold swim in the murky black water.

Several more casts resulted in more fish

which Jake released, but kept on until he had three very nice bream. That was enough for his supper and it looked like he could feast on fish about any time he wanted to.

He opened his pack and took out some Vienna sausages and saltine crackers and had his lunch. Sandy sat and begged. Jake gave her some dog biscuits and that satisfied her.

After sitting there for a few minutes enjoying the tranquility of the spot, he started east to look for the pine thicket where he could make camp. It was a little harder going since he had to dodge a lot of snags, but he could tell that someone had cleared out a small path through the swamp that made the going a little easier. He thought that Mr. Simpson must have done it to make it a little easier to get to his still. He took a wrong turn several times and had to back out and try again, but in a few minutes he saw the tall pines and knew he was on the right track.

The old man had been right. There was a nice piece of high ground that would make a nice, dry camp. Sandy bounded out of the canoe before Jake could get it pulled up on shore. She had already explored the twelve hundred square foot island in the middle of the swamp by the time Jake had secured the canoe and unpacked his gear.

Jake found the place where someone had sunk a pipe to make an artesian well that flowed off into a little stream that emptied into the swamp. Jake did not hesitate to drink some of the water and found it very refreshing.

He found the fire pit left over from the old still and began to set up his camp. Two nicely spaced trees made a perfect place to string up his jungle hammock. He set up a small lean-to where he could store his gear and found a nice place to string up his food bags to keep them away from any critters that might be coming around. Also in the lean-to he made a place where Sandy could sleep and be dry near his hammock.

He tried his cell phone, but could not get any reception. He felt very isolated, but was not concerned because he enjoyed being on his own. He checked out his camera gear and put on his best telephoto lens hoping that he would be ready when he found some woodpeckers to shoot.

He gathered enough dry firewood for the night and the next day. Time had slipped away and it was dusk when he dressed his three fish and started his supper fire. Jake was not one to skimp on his food even when he was camping. He shredded some cabbage for slaw and got out his iron skillets to cook his fish and fry his corn bread.

Sandy came nosing around to remind Jake that she wanted some of the good-smelling fish. He took one fish and carefully removed the bones and gave it to Sandy. She enjoyed the crispy fried fish and several pieces of the fried cornbread. She was not much for the slaw. By the time Jake finished eating and cleaning up the dishes, he was ready for bed. The long day of paddling and the many night sounds of the swamp quickly put him to sleep. His hammock nestling above the ground between the trees put his mind at ease; he knew that he would not have any creepy crawling things in bed with him in the morning. The last sound he remembered hearing was the call of the screech owl.

The sun shining through the leafless trees and the call of the many swamp creatures woke Jake early in the morning. The sky was bright and it looked like another beautiful day. Sandy had not even moved until Jake called her as he got out of his hammock. She slowly came over for her morning head rub, stopping to stretch her legs, as she wagged her tail to let Jake know that she was glad to see him up and about. She knew that it meant something good to eat.

As Jake was getting ready to take his breakfast food out of his grub bag, he heard a very loud "'rat-tat-tat" high in a nearby tree. He quickly picked up his binoculars and began to scan the surrounding treetops. For several minutes he did not see anything, but then he caught sight of the red plume on the bobbing head of a big woodpecker which again disappeared into the backside of the tree. He was going to have to get in his canoe and maneuver to the other side of the tree if he was going to see this bird. Sandy was right there and jumped into the bow of the boat as Jake pushed off from shore as quietly as possible with his camera and binoculars safely on board.

He maneuvered the boat in a wide circle to try to get to the backside of the tree where he had seen the woodpecker. Just as he got in range, the woodpecker flew to another tree. Still not in range for a clear picture, Jake continued to pole the boat along in the shallow water. He finally got one clear shot as the bird worked at getting his breakfast out of the bark of the tree, but when Jake moved again the bird was off to another tree further into the swamp.

When Jake looked around, he quickly realized how much the swamp looked the same everywhere. He was not sure which way to go to get back to his camp. He chided himself for not being more observant, but it would have been hard to watch for the bird and also check his landmarks. By scanning the tree tops with his binoculars, he finally made out the pine thicket which was really not where he thought it was, but he slowly poled the canoe back in that direction and in a few minutes was in a little deeper water and plainly saw the pine thicket off in the distance. It did not take him long to get back to his little island and to get back to finishing his breakfast.

After eating and feeding Sandy and getting the dishes clean and his camp back in order, he took a few minutes to study the terrain and got some bearings with his compass. He did not want the uneasy feeling of not knowing where he was again. The swamp was not a place to get lost and have to spend a night without the convenience of camp gear.

Jake packed a small daypack, got his photography gear, 410 shot gun and pistol, and then he and Sandy got back in the canoe to explore more of the swamp and to look for more evidence of the woodpeckers.

He went out to the main run of the swamp at the two cypress trees with the white rag and headed upstream again to go farther into the heart of the swamp. He flushed two wood ducks into the air as he rounded a curve and was able to get a good picture of them as they lifted off the water. The logs were filled with sunbathing turtles and they splashed into the water as he came into their view.

Further along, a cottonmouth moccasin sunning on a tree limb slid into the water. Jake was glad that he was far enough away that the snake did not slide into the boat. Out of the corner of his eye he saw two big eyes disappear under the water near the bank and knew that he had just seen the head of a gator. As he was watching the gator disappear, the canoe hit an underwater snag which threw it against a low overhanging limb, and a snake dropped into the boat. Jake quickly used his paddle to flip the snake into the water. He did not want to think about what would happen if he or Sandy got snakebit out there in the middle of nowhere. It could be a disaster. Although he knew how to take care of himself, he did not want to go through an ordeal like that.

He sat quietly in the canoe, moving very slowly with the current and listening for the woodpeckers to begin their tapping again. In a few minutes he heard tapping from two different directions indicating that there was more than one bird in the area. Jake felt good about that both from the standpoint that it might be easier to get pictures and it told him that the birds were not extent yet. He hoped there were both a male and female, but he was not sure how to tell the difference. If he could get some good pictures the experts would be able to distinguish the differences between the birds.

Jake heard some dogs barking in the distance and thought that there must be some hunters in the area, but he did not know how they would get to this place with very little dry ground.

The tapping was getting closer. He took out his binoculars and scoured the tops of the trees looking for the tell-tell red plume. For a split second he saw the plume as the bird went around the tree searching for insects. He began to move in that direction, being careful to be as quiet as possible and to look out for low-hanging limbs that might contain a sunning snake.

The woodpecker appeared and Jake got several good shots before it flew to a nearby tree. Since the bird was still in his line of sight, Jake was able to get even better pictures. Because of the bird's large size, Jake knew that he had some pictures of the Ivory-billed Woodpecker rather than its smaller version, the Pilatead Woodpecker. It made him feel good to know that he was helping to preserve this very beautiful bird.

Now what he wanted to do was to get some pictures of the two birds together. He sat still, looking and listening. Then there it was: both birds in the same tree. He practically threw down the binoculars, reaching for his camera. They almost looked like they were posing for him. One flew to a nearer tree and then the other followed. Jake got some wonderful shots. As they began to move away, Jake followed by paddling as quietly as he could.

The baying of the hounds was getting closer, which presented a mystery. What were they after and how were they moving through the mass of water and thickets? As he was thinking about this, Jake heard another distinct sound, that of a helicopter flying near by. His mind went back into his FBI mode. Putting the barking dogs and the helicopter sounds together, he reasoned that they were looking for someone. He decided that he would not let this disturb his mission of getting more information about the woodpeckers and he started moving his boat toward the woodpeckers.

After several hours and a lot of good shots, Jake decided he had better start back toward camp before it got too dark for him to find his way. He knew that the main channel was off to the east and after stopped to be sure which way the water was flowing, he began moving more to the east. In a few minutes, he broke out into the channel and kept going downstream to find the two big cypress trees with the white flag. When he found this landmark and turned toward the pine thicket, he noticed that Sandy had stood up and the hair on her back bristled.

He knew that something was wrong, but did not know what it was. He moved as quietly as he could and as he neared the pine thicket, he saw a dugout canoe pulled up on shore and two men rummaging through his gear. He reached for his shotgun and put the pistol on the floor in front of him. One man was in an orange jumpsuit and the other had taken off the jumpsuit and had put on some of Jake's clothes. Jake knew that they must be who the dogs and helicopter were searching for. The two were so busy looking for food that they did not see Jake coming through the swamp. He maneuvered the canoe behind a big cypress tree and watched for a few minutes, trying to determine if they had any guns.

"Hello the camp. Can you spare a man a cup of coffee?" Jake yelled.

He guided the canoe toward the pine thicket, watching the two men very closely to see if they had any weapons.

He had his shotgun pointed in their direction just in case they did, and he wanted to be ready when and if they started to be aggressive. Sandy just stood there looking at them and then looking back at Jake to see what he was going to do.

The two men were startled at Jake's call because they had not heard or seen Jake coming.

"We were just making some coffee. Come on in," the man in Jake's clothing hollered back at him.

Jake still did not see any weapons, but he wanted to be sure before he made his move.

He slid the canoe up to the bank, but sat still

in the canoe while he continued to take in all the surroundings. Sandy was now standing with her feet on the seat in front of her.

"What brings you boys into the swamp, hunting or fishing?" Jake asked.

"We were going to fish some," the man in the orange jumpsuit answered.

"I like your boat. It looks like one a friend of mine had. How did you come by that?" Jake asked.

"A friend let us use it to come fishing."

"What is your friend's name?" Jake asked.

"Billy Jones," the man wearing Jake's clothes sputtered out.

"I don't think so. Where is the man who owns that boat?" Jake asked angrily, raising the shotgun to where the men could see it.

"You are lying through your teeth. You are in my camp, wearing my clothes, and have stolen Nash Odom's boat. What happened to Nash?"

"We left him back in the swamp. He told us about this island."

"Did you hurt him?" Jake asked, getting madder all the time.

"Naw, but that does not mean we will not hurt you."

The two men started to move apart and one of them reached behind his back and pulled out a pistol. Before he could aim at Jake, Sandy leaped out of the boat and lunged at the man, knocking him to the ground. He dropped the gun. When the other man reached for it, Jake fired a shot at the ground in front of him with his pistol.

"Nice work, Sandy. I did not know you had it in you." Jimbo must have taught you that when I was not around, Jake thought. "I told you not to try anything stupid and the next shot will be through that hard heart of yours. Sandy, come here."

Sandy, still snarling and showing her teeth, came back to Jake. "Move away from the gun and get down on your knees."

Jake picked up the gun, went to his pack and got a length of rope, and tied the two men back to back around one of the large pine trees.

"How long have you been in the swamp?"

"Two days. We escaped from a clean-up crew."

"You must have wanted to get away pretty bad to come into this swamp."

"Some buddies were supposed to meet us, but they never showed. When we found the old man and his boat we thought we had it made. We were going to get into the river and just disappear. Who are you?"

"I'm Jake Johnson. I used to work for the FBI, but now I take wildlife pictures. Glad I was here to help you boys out before the gators got you."

"What are you going to do with us?"

"Well, I am going to give you something to eat and then we will wait here until the authorities come or I will take you out by myself."

Jake fried up some bacon, scrambled some powdered eggs and made a pot of coffee which he shared with the two men.

Every ten minutes or so, Jake would fire a shot into the air, hoping that the authorities would hear it and come his way. In a few minutes, Jake saw Sandy stand up and peer off into the swamp. Shortly after, he saw two boats come toward the pine thicket.

"I'm Jake Johnson and I have your two fugitives."

As the boats approached the pine thicket, Jake recognized Nash Odom and yelled to him, "Glad to see that you are all right, Nash."

"I'm fine, but those two fellows stole my boat and I hooked up with the authorities to help track them down. Glad you and Sandy are all right."

"We had a little excitement for a few minutes, but I got everything under control with Sandy's help."

The three deputies were now out of the boat and untied the two escapees, putting handcuffs on them to take them back out of the swamp. They reported on their radio that they had the two escapees, were coming out, and in about two hours would be at the point where the swamp empties into the river,

"I would like to get my clothes back from that fellow," Jake said to one of the deputies.

"Sure thing," he replied as he got the orange jumpsuit and had the fellow change clothes.

"What are you doing in the swamp?" the other deputy asked Jake.

"Looking to take some pictures of big

woodpeckers. Hope all the excitement did not scare them away. I have some pictures, but hope to get some better ones. I'm working for the Wildlife Resources Commission."

"You be careful, this swamp can be a dangerous place. We saw a couple of gators as we came your way."

"We will be fine. Nash, you haven't changed your mind about staying with me, have you?"

'No, I had better go see if I can get a deer. My buddies won't wait too long for me. Glad to have my boat back. It has been in my family for a long time."

After having a cup of Jake's coffee, the deputies asked Nash to lead them back out of the swamp before it got too dark. Jake and Nash shook hands, saying that they would see each other another time as the three boats headed back out of the swamp.

Jake and Sandy stood on the small island in the middle of the swamp and watched the three boats until they were out of sight. When they were gone, Jake went to the fire pit and stirred up the fire, bringing it back to life so he could cook his supper.

After a few minutes with his fly rod, he had enough perch for a nice meal for him and Sandy. He fried them up very crispy, made slaw, and fried some cornbread. Then he and Sandy sat down to a delicious meal. The night sounds were beginning as the sun sank lower and lower. Twilight took over prior to the pitch dark of the swamp at night. The night sky was filled with stars as Jake prepared to bed down in his hammock. Sandy lay by the fire until it was gone and then curled up under the tent Jake had set up for her.

The two hardly stirred until the sun started peaking through the trees with the making of another beautiful day. Sandy came over and stood looking up at Jake as if to say, get up sleepy head, the day is passing us by.

As he lay there, Jake could hear woodpeckers tapping away in the distance and that stirred him to get up and get ready for another day of chasing them through the swamp. With some luck, this might be the last day he would need. He already had a lot of very good shots of what he thought were males and females to show that they were thriving in the area. He would be looking for a nesting tree today to see if there were any young ones around.

After a quick breakfast of oatmeal and bacon, he and Sandy headed out. This time he set his GPS so that no matter how far away he got, he could return to camp without the possibility of having to spend another night in the swamp away from camp.

When Jake was finally ready, Sandy was already sitting in the boat waiting for him. He shoved off from shore and headed toward the tapping sound he heard in the distance. After about thirty minutes of steady paddling, he found himself back in the run of the swamp and headed up against the slow-moving current until he found where another stream was emptying into the run of the swamp and headed up that little creek, still following the tap-tap of the woodpeckers. In a few minutes he was in the middle of a stand of very big cypress trees. As he stopped his boat in an eddy, he began to see flashes of red moving around on a big cypress. He got several more clear shots and saw two other birds that were smaller than the others and knew that he had found their nesting area. Checking his GPS he made a note so he could alert the wildlife folks where the nesting site was. They were looking to put up a webcam if they could find the nesting area. Jake had gotten the information they needed, and decided it was time to head back to camp and try to get out of the swamp before dark.

The slight current plus Jake's hard paddling got him back into the main run, and before long he was headed straight back to his island.

He had everything pretty much in order and it did not take him long to stow everything in the boat and lash it down. Then he and Sandy were headed back to civilization. The swamp was very different from the mountains, but had a beauty of its own. On the way back to the main river, Jake saw two deer and an otter along with logs full of turtles, and two eyes that quickly disappeared underwater as he rounded the bend. He got pictures of the deer and otter, but the alligator was too quick for him and he decided not to stay around to see if it would surface again.

Out on the river Jake headed downstream and

in a little while he was pulling his boat up on the sandy shore of Queen Anne's Landing. He brought his pick-up around from the parking lot and loaded his gear and boat in the back. As the sun set, he and Sandy headed back to Lumberton for another night at the motel. After checking in, he decided that he would go to Fuller's for supper. He loved their large buffet of almost any country food a person could want, from fried cornbread to fried fatback with the biggest selection of home-cooked vegetables that he had ever seen outside of a Sunday after church feeding on the grounds. He literally prepared a doggy bag to take back for Sandy and knew that she would love it.

Back at the motel after Sandy had devoured the goodies he had brought her, they took a long walk and ended up downtown. Jake ambled along through the downtown remembering things from his youth and wishing some of the stores he had frequented as a boy were still there. He stopped outside the refurbished Carolina Theater and read of coming attractions. This theater was the place to be on Saturday nights for the late show when he was growing up. When he was a kid the Saturday afternoon matinee cowboy shows were preceded by an exciting serial which was designed to bring the audience back each week to find out what would happen next. He could still see Red Ryder and Little Beaver, who once put on a stage show in that very theater. But times had changed and he had also changed.

A notice on the marquee caught his eye and triggered a memory. He had heard his mom talk about Nathan Moyer, a young man she had taught in Sunday School who wanted to be a concert pianist. Here he was. He took out his cell phone and called his mom.

"Hello there. This is Jake."

"Hello, dear. Where are you?"

"I am in Lumberton and guess what?"

"What?"

"Nathan Moyer is going to be giving a performance at the Carolina Theater here in Lumberton tonight. It is called "Celebrating the Bicentennial of Franz Liszt,' I think I will stay another night and attend the performance."

"You will love it. He is so gifted."

"If I get a chance to speak to him, I will remember you to him."

"Tell him I am proud of him and wish I was there."

"Goodbye Mom. Tell Dad hello."

Jake and Sandy returned to the motel and had a nice night in a soft, comfortable bed. Jake was in no hurry to get up and slept later than usual. He decided he would spend what was left of the day on the river. He spent part of it using his metal detector to try to find some old coins around the old pavilion site at McMillian's beach. The rest of the afternoon was consumed in looking for shark's teeth in the sandy parts of the bends of the river. He managed to find four whole ones and some broken pieces; along with the three dollars and fifty-four cents he had found at the old beach area he felt like he had had a successful day.

After another good evening meal at Fuller's, he was at the theater in time to get a good seat. He was pleased with the turnout and enjoyed a very relaxing time of listening to beautiful piano music. He was impressed by the expression that Nathan put into his music. Jackie had been the driving force behind their attendance at concerts, but he had learned to appreciate music and had gotten beyond thinking a concert was just a nice place to take a relaxing nap.

After the performance, he had a chance to talk to Nathan, who was delighted that he had bothered to come, and was very pleased that Mrs. Johnson had been a fan for such a long time.

Jake and Sandy were up early and after a quick breakfast they were on the road to Ocean Isle Beach. Jake rolled down the window and Sandy was in dog heaven with her head out the window and her short coat blowing in the wind. Every now and then she would look over at Jake as if to say thank you.

He had an early lunch at Melvin's, where he enjoyed chatting with the people in line. As usual he was able to talk to someone who had a Lumberton connection. While in the vicinity, he decided to drive around White Lake and see how it had changed over the years. Camp Chicagami where he had worked as a counselor had been replaced with lake houses. The old FFA camp was still there. He saw no sign of the old glass bottom boats that used to take people on cruises around the lake. Like everywhere else there had been a lot of new building on every square inch of lakefront property. He was glad he had seen it when it was a more pristine place.

Before he realized it, he was pulling into his driveway at Ocean Isle.

CHAPTER 26

THE ALABAMA THEATER WITH SUSAN

FRIDAY, JUNE 6, 2003

Before going upstairs, Jake unloaded his gear into the storage room and hung the canoe he had bought from the Forest Service underneath the cottage. Sandy made her rounds to check everything out and then bounded up the stairs after Jake.

He poured himself a Grape Crush over ice and took his phone on the porch to watch the sun set and to check in with the world. His first call was to Barbara, and since she was not available, he left her a message to call when she could. John picked up the phone on the first ring and knew that it was Jake calling.

"You back from you bird-watching trip?"

"Yeah, just got back and am enjoying the nice

breeze on my porch. What have you been up to?"

"Working on catching the bad guys, but your bad guy has not shown up on the radar yet."

"He still has a bone to pick with me so he will eventually show up. I am actually looking forward to it. I want to get it over with."

"Have you talked to Barbara?"

"Could not reach her, but left her a message. Do you know where she is?"

"Malcolm sent her out to California to work on a case for a few days. She should be back in the office tomorrow. Am sure she will call as soon as she gets your message. She was asking me when you were to get back."

"I'm getting a beep. Might be Barbara. Talk to you later."

"Hello," Jake said as he pushed the button to take the incoming call.

"Hello yourself," Susan said to a surprised Jake, who was expecting Barbara.

"Well, good to hear from you."

"I saw your truck was back as I went home from work, so I thought I would give you a call. How was your trip into the wilds of Big Swamp?"

"We got some good pictures of the woodpeckers and Sandy and I managed to capture two escaped jailbirds in the process, so we had an exciting time. We are both glad to be home with some modern conveniences. Anything new with you?"

"Ricky, the comedian at the Alabama Theater, is going to give his own show on Saturday night. I have an extra ticket. Would you like to go with me?"

"I have heard he is really good, but I have never seen him in person. I would love to go."

"I'll pick you up about four and we can have supper at Calabash before we go to the show."

"That sounds great. Don't you want me to drive?"

"You can drive, but my car is more comfortable than your pick-up."

"That's fine, see you on Saturday."

That is a difference between Barbara and Susan, Jake thought as he hung up the phone. Barbara would have been just as comfortable in a pick-up as she would have been in a car. He enjoyed being with both of them, but there were a lot of subtle differences. One day he would have to make a choice between the two, but right now he was enjoying them both as long as their paths did not cross.

Jake spent some time working on his pictures and printing out those that he wanted to present to the Wildlife Commission. He also prepared pictures of the poachers to send to Ron for their trial.

Susan pulled into the drive about two minutes to four on Saturday and Jake was ready. He had already taken care of Sandy. He set his alarms as he went out the door and Susan was getting out of the car and getting ready to change seats as he came down the stairs. Jake opened the door for her and gave her a hug and she kissed him on the cheek.

On the drive to Calabash, they talked over their week and brought each other up to date on what had been happening. After a little discussion, they decided on Dockside and in a few moments were seated at a table overlooking the river. They enjoyed the hush puppies while waiting for their meal. They were engrossed in small talk and Susan was impressed with Jake's being able to capture the two convicts. She was interested in seeing his photos and asked if she might have some of them for her museum. He assured her that after the Wildlife people took their pick, she could have the rest.

They arrived at the theater in plenty of time and found their seats, and settled in for an entertaining night. Ricky did not disappoint them and Jake had not laughed so much in a long time. Susan enjoyed seeing him having such a good time.

As they drove through the backcountry on the way back to Ocean Isle, Jake pointed out several deer grazing along the roadside and nearly had to stop to keep from hitting a possum that was crossing the road.

When they arrived back at Better Than Nutting Jake invited Susan in for a cup of hot chocolate.

"Any marshmallows? She asked.

"Sure, what is hot chocolate without marshmallows"?

Sandy was glad to see them as Jake let her out, but she did not stay outside long because she did not want to miss anything. Susan always paid her plenty of attention and she reveled in it.

Jake and Susan sat on the porch enjoying the breeze, the conversation, and listening to the waves pound the shore. Susan finally said that she had to go because she had to leave early for Raleigh the next day.

"I need to take Sandy for a little run. We could ride to your place with you and then we could jog back if you don't mind Sandy riding in your fancy car."

"Heavens no," Susan replied with a big smile.

"Let me change and I will be right out."

When they reached Susan's place, Jake walked her to the door and told her how much he had enjoyed the evening and really appreciated her sharing the tickets with him.

"If I did not have to be up so early in the morning we could enjoy it a little longer, but we can make it up later."

Susan petted Sandy who had managed to squeeze between them and Jake gave Susan a hug and a kiss and told her goodnight.

Sandy was reluctant to leave, but she finally followed Jake down the stairs and fell into a trot beside him as he jogged back toward his cottage.
It was a nice night and he enjoyed the exercise and stopped several times to let Sandy explore a little.

Very few people were out and Jake was startled as a car pulled up behind him and the blue light of the city patrol car flashed.

"Hello Jake," Dan called out as he rolled down the squad car window.

Jake went over and leaned into the window and shook hands with Dan.

"Good to have you back on the island. How was your trip to Big Swamp? Already heard that you helped catch the two runaways."

"Yeah, they were messing with my camp and Sandy did not like that. You should have seen her take one of them down. I did not know she had it in her."

"Did you and Susan enjoy Ricky tonight?"

"I forgot that you know everything that is going on. Yeah, he is really good. Don't know when I have laughed so much."

"We heard from John. Still no news about John Wesley. We kept an eye on your place while you were gone."

"Thanks."

The radio squeaked and Dan said, "Got to go. A little fender bender over at the stoplight. See you later."

Jake waved as the squad car moved away with its lights flashing. Hope he does not have another wreck. He sure gets excited about things, Jake thought.

Back at the cottage Jake took a shower and was soon slipping off to sleep as the waves pounded the sand like a sweet lullaby.

CHAPTER 27

DEADLY VISITOR

SATURDAY, JUNE 7, 2003

Hearing Sandy's low growl next to his bed awakened Jake. Jake.heard footsteps on the gravel underneath the cottage and bounded out of bed. In an instant he and Sandy disappeared down the hidden stairway into his safe room. He immediately switched on his monitors and saw a shadowy figure slowly going up the stairs with a pistol in his outstretched hand.

Jake pushed a button on his control panel that sent a signal to the police station. The intruder paused at the door long enough to pick the old lock, and then he was inside. Jake pushed a second button that set the automatic locks on both the front and back doors. The intruder quickly moved toward Jake's bedroom and fired two rapid shots into what

234

he thought was Jake lying in the bed. Because of the silencer on the gun, Jake could barely hear what had happened, but he had it recorded in his system. The man reached over and pulled back the cover to find a wadded up pillow with two holes where Jake's head would have been.

He kicked the bed, whirled around and proceeded to search the house. When he couldn't find Jake or Sandy, he started for the door, but found it locked. He went to the front of the house and tried that door and it was also locked and no matter how hard he tried he could not get it open.

Jake picked up a police radio and said, "This is Jake Johnson. There is an armed man in my house. Be extremely careful. Sandy and I are outside the house."

Just as he finished speaking Jake heard a crash as a chair went through the picture window in the living room. He picked up his 410 shotgun and opened the door that let him go into the outdoor shower.

The man was running down the stairs as Jake came out of the shower and stepped in front of him, knocking him off balance, but not before the man got off a shot that went wild.

As he reached for the gun lying on the ground, Jake said, "Don't do it. My next shot will be to kill you and I don't think you are ready to meet your maker."

Jake heard, in the distance, the police siren heading his way.

"The police are on the way. Who are you and what are you doing shooting up my house and breaking out my windows? Did John Wesley send you?"

There was no answer from the man who continued to cuss Jake and holler in pain from his busted knee caused by the fall.

Dan pulled up in the squad car with the lights flashing and got out with his drawn gun.

"Dan, it's me, Jake Johnson. I have the man down over here."

"What happened and who is he?"

"He broke into my house and put two bullets into my pillow, and then broke out the picture window trying to escape, but I do not know who he is."

Dan asked him for ID and then put handcuffs on him and took him to the squad car.

"His name is Jes Ramsey and there is a warrant out for his arrest."

"Does he have any connections with John Wesley William's?"

"I don't know, but we will try to find out. I am going to take him to the station and lock him up until the chief can get there."

"I will come over later. I need to do something about the broken window."

"We will get a full statement from you later."

"You might want to take a picture of the pillow and dig the two slugs out of the mattress. You did pick up his gun, didn't you?" Jake said to Dan.

"How did he miss you?"

"Sandy heard him coming and I got out of the room."

Jake did not mention the safe room because he did not want anyone to know about it yet.

Jake got a big piece of plastic and a staple gun and put it over the broken window. He got the broom and dustpan and swept up as much glass as he could and then ran the vacuum cleaner over the rug. Most of the glass was on the outside porch.

Jake decided he was not going to be able to sleep so he made some breakfast, fed Sandy, and headed over to the police station. It was too early to call John and Malcolm, but he was sure they would want to know about this. It had to be related to John Wesley.

The chief had arrived at the station and he and Dan were questioning Mr. Ramsey when Jake arrived. The chief motioned for Jake to come into the room. The hair on Sandy's neck bristled when she saw Mr. Ramsey and she let out a low growl.

"You had better stay out here, girl," Jake said to Sandy as he entered the room where the three men were.

"Jake, you sure bring some excitement to the island," the chief said as Jake entered the room.

"Is that good or bad, Chief?"

"When we are usually concerned with people littering and speeding, attempted murder does bring something else to the table."

"Found out anything else about Mr. Ramsey?"

"He won't own up to knowing John Wesley,

but we suspect there is a connection there somewhere."

"Since he is wanted in two other states, we have contacted the FBI," Dan said.

"I haven't called Malcolm or John yet, but they are going to be interested in him."

When Jake asked Mr. Ramsey if he had anything to say, he just stared at Jake.

"Dan is going to take him to Bolivia to put him in the county jail until the FBI can get here."

"Can I have a few minutes with him before he goes?" Jake asked the chief.

"You are not going to do anything stupid, are you Jake?"

"No, I just want to have a little conversation with him."

"While Dan is finishing up some paper work I will let you talk to him."

When Dan and the chief left, Jake sat down at the table across from Mr. Ramsey and glared at him.

"I know that you are working for John Wesley Williams or the man who hired him and I just want to send them a message. I am tired of this and the next person who comes to see me might not be as lucky as you. John Wesley is not going to get his money back and I am going to get the man behind all this and when I do I hope there is someone else with me to keep me from ending it all right then and there. You be sure to get the message to them through your lawyer and I hope you spend a long time in jail."

The man did not say a word or change his expression. He just stared at Jake as Jake got up from the table and left the room.

"Chief, is it all right if I ride with Dan to take the prisoner to Bolivia?"

"Sure, I am sure Dan would like the company."

"Can Sandy stay here until I get back?"

"Sure, she usually makes herself at home here anyway."

Dan took the prisoner, put him in the back seat of the squad car, and told Jake they were ready to go.

Just as they were going over the high-rise bridge back to the mainland, Jake's phone rang.

Jake looked at the display and saw that it was John calling.

"Good morning, John. You are up early."

"Not as early as you, I understand. You OK?"

"Sandy, my early warning system, alerted me and we were gone by the time the man fired the two shots into my pillow."

"Thank God for Sandy. Malcolm has Barbara and me on the way down there to escort Mr. Ramsey to federal prison and to see if we can find any connection to John Wesley. That bad boy is still on the loose."

"You had better find him before I do. I am getting fed up with him and I will not feel at ease until he is dead or behind bars. When are you arriving?"

"We get into Wilmington at two and we will

see you about four at Ocean Isle. We will stay at your place if that is all right. We need to talk to the prisoner before we get there."

"That is fine. Hope to have the window fixed by then. Tell Barbara hello for me and I look forward to seeing you both."

As Jake hung up, the chief called Dan on the radio.

"Dan, this is the Chief. In looking at Mr. Ramsey's car, which was parked down the street, I found a receipt from the Holiday Inn. On your way back from Bolivia you and Jake check it out to see what he might have left in his room."

"Will do, Chief."

Jake turned around and said to Ramsey, "Hope you left John Wesley there. That would make it almost too easy."

The rest of the short ride to Bolivia went pretty much in silence with just some small talk between Jake and Dan.

When they deposited Ramsey at the jail, Jake told Dan to tell the officials not to let Ramsey talk to anyone until they had a chance to check out the motel room. "We do not want to spook anyone if there is someone waiting for him."

Dan and Jake left the jail, and went back to Ocean Isle, and stopped at the Holiday Inn on Highway 17.

When Dan entered the lobby, he said, "Hello Chuck, haven't seen you in a while. This is Jake Johnson. We need to check on a couple of your guests."

"Official business, is it?"

"Yeah. We don't know if they are still here or not."

"Who are you looking for?"

"Jes Ramsey."

Chuck went to his computer and entered a few keystrokes and said, "Yeah, he checked in late last night. He is in room 211."

"Was there anyone with him?"

'No, he had a single room, but another fellow came in about the same time. They did not say anything to each other, but I got the feeling they were together."

"What was his name?"

After a few more keystrokes Chuck said, "He paid cash and I did not see any ID, but he registered as Les Catlin. He was in room 224."

"Is he still here?"

"He has not checked out and I have not seen him this morning."

"We need to check out those two rooms. Can you let us in?"

Chuck picked up a master key and yelled to someone in the back to come handle the front desk.

"We need to see Catlin's room first." Dan said as they get off the elevator.

"Knock on the door to see if he is in his room," Dan said to Chuck.

Chuck knocked on the door and said, "Hotel management, Mr. Catlin are you there?"

There was no answer and Dan motioned to

Chuck to open the door as he pulled out his revolver. Chuck stepped out of the way and Dan and Jake entered the room with drawn guns. They checked the bathroom, but there was no one there. The suitcase was still there and there were toiletries in the bathroom.

"Looks like he is planning to come back," Jake said.

"Let's check the other room," Dan replied.

Chuck moved to the other room and knocked on the door. There was no answer.

"Open the door," Dan said.

They entered the room with guns drawn. There was no one there, but the room still appeared to be occupied.

"Looks like he plans to return also," Dan said as his radio activated and the chief said, "Where are you?"

"Jake and I are at the motel, but no one is here."

"Who are you looking for? I thought you took Mr. Ramsey to jail."

"We did. We think he had someone with him, but he is not in his motel room."

"That might be because I am holding him here at the station. He was walking down the street and when I stopped to ask him a question, he bolted and I had to chase him down. He says his name is Les Catlin, but he does not have any ID on him."

"That is the name that he used to check into the motel."

"Jake and I will be right there."

"Tell the clerk to seal the two room, and not to let anyone in."

While Dan was on the radio with the chief, Jake rummaged through the suitcase and came up with two driver's licenses. "One is Les Catlin from Vegas and the other is Bob Young from Black Rock, North Carolina."

"I am going to take these to the chief," Jake said to Dan.

"Chuck, seal these two rooms and do not let anyone in. We will be back to gather up this stuff and will see that their bills are paid. We will send some boys form the crime lab to check them out thoroughly."

As they were getting into the car, Jake said, "Sure thought one of these two would be John Wesley. Wonder if this is connected with him or has something else from my past brought this on?"

Back at the station the chief said, "Even if this fellow is not part of the threat on Jake's life, he has some outstanding warrants we can hold him with. Did you find anything at the motel?"

"Just these two driver's licenses," Jake said as he handed them to the chief.

"Dan, call the lab boys and have them go over the two rooms. They might be able to find something. Are your FBI friends still coming down?"

"As far as I know. I think they will still be interested in these two fellows. If you don't need me, I am going back to the house. I have some things I need to take care of."

"Fine. We will let you know if we find out anything else."

As he was walking back to the house, his phone rang and it was John.

"Where are you?" Jake asked.

"We are getting off the plane in Wilmington. I have some news for you. Barbara is not with me. She got called away at the last minute and Malcolm sent Jeannie with me. Can you accommodate both of us at your place?"

"Sure, it will be good to see her again. Did she bring her diving gear?" Jake asked, laughing.

"No, but she was talking about wanting to dive with you again. She does have her photograph album of her dive with you in the Caymans. We are going to stop in Bolivia and talk to the prisoner. We should be at Ocean Isle in about two hours."

"Look forward to seeing you."

Jake remembered how he and Jeannie had met in the Caymans when Malcolm had sent her to watch over him and he did not know it. He had just thought that a good-looking girl had taken an interest in him. He wondered if he could juggle three women at one time. He still missed Jackie, but bachelorhood still had its good times, he thought as he smiled to himself.

He got the cottage ready for his guest. Just as he was about to sit down for a little rest, he heard a vehicle in his driveway and saw that it was the glass company that had come to fix his window.

"Hello, I am Jake. Glad you could get here so

soon," he said as he opened the door and greeted the workmen.

"We have your new tinted glass and we should be able to get it in this afternoon."

"That will be great. I am having guests in a couple of hours."

"We should be through by then and have you all set. How did the window get broken?"

"I had a break-in and he threw a chair through the window. He is in jail now. I put that plastic over it because I did not know how long it would take you to get here. If I can help with anything, let me know."

The workmen prepared the window frame for the new glass and in a few minutes they brought the replacement glass up the stairs.

"Think you are going to like this new tinted gas-filled glass. It will help with the heating and cooling and cut out almost all of the glare," the workman said to Jake as they fitted it into place. "As long as it does not mess up my view, it will be fine."

"I believe that it will even make it better. You really do have a nice view."

They cleaned up all the mess, got Jake to sign the bill, and they were on their way, leaving Jake impressed by the efficiency in which they came and did their job.

Jake got a Vernor's ginger ale from the fridge and a pack of nabs and sat down to wait for Jeannie and John. Sandy licked up the crumbs that fell to the floor as Jake finished off his snack.

Just about as he was ready to doze off, he heard a car in the driveway and Sandy gave a low bark and went to the back door. By the time Jake got there, John and Jeannie were coming up the stairs with bags in their hands.

"Hello there friends," Jake said as he opened the door for them. He shook John's hand and gave Jeannie a big hug as he took her bag and ushered them into the house. Sandy nuzzled up to Jeannie as if to say, I don't know you, but I would like to be friends. Jeannie kneeled down and petted Sandy like she had known her a long time.

Jake thought that maybe she had already endeared herself to Sandy, in the hope that he would be next. Jake showed his two guests to their rooms, and in a few minutes Jeannie came out with a book in her hand.

"Jake, this is a house-warming gift for you. I picked it up at the airport. Hope you will like it. It reminded me of our time in the Caymans."

Jake thanked her and saw that the book was about shipwrecks off the coast of Ocean Isle.

"This should be interesting. I have wanted to do some diving, but have not gotten around to it yet. Maybe we can get in a dive before you leave," Jake said as he smiled and gave Jeannie another big hug, thanking her again for the book.

"I did bring my pictures from the Cayman trip. I kind of hated it that I was there spying on you, but you taught me a lot about photography in those two days."

"Well, you were just doing your job and did it well because I did not even suspect a thing. I just enjoyed being with a beautiful girl," Jake said, making her blush.

John came out of his room looking like a tourist and asking, "Where are we going for supper? I am ready for some more good North Carolina sea food."

"We can go back to Calabash - you seemed to like that."

"Sounds great. Jeannie, have you ever been to Calabash?"

"No. This is my first trip to North Carolina. If John is going casual I will too," and she left the room to change out of her traveling clothes.

Jake and John caught up a little and Jake found out that they did not really get any information out of the prisoners. There did not seem to be any connection to John Wesley Williams, but they could not find out why they were after Jake.

Jake and John had to concentrate on keeping their mouths from dropping open when Jeannie appeared out of her bedroom wearing black leather pants slung low with flair legs and an angora-blend sweater with funnel neck and half sleeves that brought out her every curve. Jake had really forgotten how attractive she had been in her swimwear when he was with her in the Caymans. She was certainly overdressed for Calabash, but neither John nor Jake was going to say anything to her. They were just going to enjoy the evening watching her being stared at by all the male patrons and frowned at by all the female patrons.

They had a fun evening, and enjoyed the good North Carolina seafood, and were able to catch up on people and events. Jake missed some of that, When he really thought about it he liked the freedom he now experienced and actually enjoyed being alone in the wild with his nature photography; yet there was still a lot of detective left in him.

Back at the cottage, Jeannie got out her photograph album and she and Jake enjoyed sharing their adventure with John. They laughed a lot about Jake not knowing he was being watched because he was so much enjoying being with such an attractive lady.

John thumbed through the Ocean Isle Beach shipwreck book that Jeannie had brought to Jake and said, "Looks like there is a wreck about three hundred yards out right in front of your cottage.

"Let me see that. I was not aware that a wreck was out there that close," Jake said.

"Could we get to it from here?" Jeannie asked.

"Yes, that is surely doable. Are you going to have any time that would allow us to make the dive?"

"Depends on what turn our investigation takes. What do you think, John?"

"It surely will take another day and that puts us to Friday. You could take the weekend and make the dive."

"Are you interested, Jake?" Jeannie asked excitedly?

"Sure." Jake said, remembering quickly how Jeannie had looked in her diving outfit in the Caymans. "There is a dive shop in town where we could rent some equipment. We could use a rubber raft and paddle out to the wreck from the shore or we could rent a boat. Which do you prefer?"

"Taking the raft sounds like fun, but I know it would be a little more work."

"Would depend on the wind and tides, but I am game to try it."

John decided to take Sandy for her evening walk while Jeannie and Jake made plans for their dive. When he returned they retired for the night with Jeannie very excited about being able to dive with Jake again.

Jake had a pancake breakfast waiting for them when John and Jeannie returned from their morning run.

"The beach is so beautiful," Jeannie said as she sat down at the table and devoured her glass of orange juice in one big gulp.

"I can see why you like it down here," John replied.

"Sandy and I have really enjoyed it, but things keep happening that keep me from enjoying the peace and quiet of the beach. The people here are real nice, and everything that has happened has caused me to enjoy good relations with the police chief and his staff."

Jake kept the pancakes coming until Jeannie and John pushed back from the table and said they had had enough. In a few minutes they were all ready to start their day of police work again, and left the cottage to go to the police station. When Jake was getting into the car, Susan pulled up on her way to work, not knowing that Jake had company.

"Good morning, Jake, You are out early."

"Yes, my friends from the FBI are down investigating the shooting. Come meet them."

Jeannie and John got out of the car and Jake made the introductions, wondering how all this was going to play out when Barbara found out about it. After a few minutes of small talk, Susan excused herself and the three got back in the car and headed for the police station.

Dan was at the station and was enamored when he met Jeannie. He almost ignored Jake and John as he showed her around the station. In a few minutes the chief came in and Jake introduced him to Jeannie. He was much more subtle than Dan, but had a hard time keeping his eyes off Jeannie. Jake and John looked on with amazement.

"Jake, we have some interesting news. We have connected our two fellows with Jimmy Spivey, the fellow who killed Mr. Farmer. Evidently you made him real mad and he sent these two to do you in. There is no connection we can find that links him with John Wesley Williams at all."

"Well, that is good news and bad news," John said. "We were hoping to get a lead on John Wesley. His trail is getting a little cold. But we are glad that you caught these two before they could carry out their plans."

"They broke out a perfectly good window and messed up a very good pillow, but gave us a reason to get two more thugs off the street." Jake said.

John's phone rang. He excused himself and left the room to talk to Malcolm. He returned in a few minute and said, "Malcolm has verified from the information that was sent to the FBI that the chief's findings are correct. They cannot find any link to Williams either and that kind of takes the FBI out of the case. He wants us back in the office on Monday."

Jake and Jeannie smiled at each other, knowing that this would allow time for their dive on Saturday. After listening to the chief and Dan sing Jake's praises, the three left the station and got back to the cottage where Jeannie and Jake began to firm up their plans for the dive. John retired to the porch with a good book and Sandy joined him, getting petted while John read and rocked in the beautiful atmosphere of the North Carolina coast.

By evening, Jake and Jeannie had collected their gear and had their plans mapped out for the dive. Jake treated them to a Frogmore Stew for supper and found two more converts to a really simple delicious meal. After supper they sat on the porch, talking and rocking and enjoying the cool breeze.

CHAPTER 28

DIVE ON THE MUDHEN

SATURDAY, JUNE 7, 2003

Jake and Jeannie were up early and had made the final adjustment on their gear when John got up. He was content to stay at the cottage and keep Sandy company, serving as their back up if needed. Jake showed him how to use the radio to keep in touch with them and gave him some emergency numbers in case they were needed.

Wearing wetsuits with their gear stowed in the raft, they pulled the raft onto the beach and into the water. They waved to John as they paddled out through the light surf and were quickly beyond the breakers and bobbing in the small swells as the early morning beach walkers gathered to watch them off, not knowing what they were doing.

Jake checked his GPS and made a correction

in their course as the raft glided smoothly through the water. It did not take them long to reach the spot. They anchored the raft in about thirty feet of water and put on their diving gear with each one checking the other's gear before they got into the water. Jake checked in with John and told him they would contact him again in about an hour.

"I'll splash first and then you follow," Jake said to Jeannie when they both were ready.

Jake was pleased with the clearness of the water and felt like it would be a good dive. He was a little surprised that this wreck was in only about thirty feet of water. The information he had read indicated that most of the wrecks were in water ninety feet or more in depth.

Even in her wetsuit Jeannie was nice to watch as she glided smoothly through the water. They could see the swirling mass of brightly colored fish as they neared the wreck. The fish were not as colorful as they had been in the Caymans, but they were still amazing to watch. Jeannie already had her camera out and was taking pictures as they went along. They both had a collection bag and Jake had his spear gun just in case any sharks got too friendly.

As they approached the boat, they could see the old anchor partially covered in the sand and the ship's bell looking like it could be rung at any time.

There was not much left of the 1800's four-masted schooner, but they could still make out what it had been. They did not venture into the gaping hole in the side of the boat, but it had allowed the contents to be spread out in the sand beside the boat. There were bottles and pots and pans and various other objects that the salt water had preserved.

Jeannie gave a thumbs up as she photographed a barracuda that swam from inside the hull. They circled the ship to see what else they might see. The metal portholes had come loose from the ship and were lying in the sand. The block and tackle from the main boom was still intact, but the rope had probably been eaten away by sea creatures. When Jake circled the boat again a small chest caught his eye. It was three-quarters buried in the sand and was hardly recognizable as a wooden chest that was mostly gone, with just the metal straps holding a little of the wood. It looked like it had just recently been uncovered by the ocean currents.

Jake began to brush away the sand and to his surprise he began to see some gold coins and some copper Indianhead pennies. He motioned for Jeannie to come and the two of them filled their collection bags with coins, but had to leave most of them behind because of the weight. Jake took out his GPS and marked the spot, hoping to come back at some future time and retrieve more of the coins.

They had been down about forty-five minutes when Jake pointed at his watch and then pointed up to let Jeannie know that it was time to surface. They made their way back to the anchor rope and slowly ascended so they would come up near the raft. When they surfaced, they could tell that the weather had changed and it looked like a storm was approaching from the east.

"We had better head for shore. We don't want to be out here in a storm in this little raft," Jake said as he threw his collection into the bottom of the raft and climbed in over the side. He helped Jeannie back into the raft and they both removed their diving gear and started paddling toward shore. The wind was in their favor and it did not take them very long to reach shore.

John and Sandy were waiting for them. Sandy swam out a little to meet them, but Jake motioned her back to the shore rather than take her into the raft. John helped them pull the raft back to the cottage and they just made it before the storm hit.

"Did you have a good dive?" John finally asked. They had been so busy getting back to the cottage, no one had said anything.

"We sure did," Jake and Jeannie blurted almost together.

"Wait 'til you see what we found," Jeannie said as she struggled to get out of her wetsuit. It was hard for Jake and John to concentrate on what she was saying as she emerged in a very revealing bikini, but she pulled her collection bag out of the raft and showed the coins to John.

"Good gracious," John exclaimed, "I did not think you would find anything like that."

"Neither did I," Jake answered.

"We had to leave a lot behind because of the

weight," Jeannie explained. "Wish we had more time to go back."

"Maybe another day," Jake said. "Might be better if we did not tell anyone else about our find. After we eat lunch I want to go to the library and see what I can find about that wreck."

"Why go to the library?" Jeannie asked, "We probably can find just as much information on our computers."

The unexpected storm struck just as they had put away their gear and headed upstairs. The wind and lightning were fierce and they could hear the pounding waves as they walked up the stairs to get inside.

Jeannie excused herself to take a shower. John and Sandy stared out the window at the raging storm. Jake got out some food for lunch and when it was all on the table he went to take his shower.

When Jake returned, John was seated at the table enjoying a nice spread of sandwich fixings with Sandy at his side waiting for him to let something fall from the table.

Jeannie was so excited about the coins she could not eat. She was busy at the computer trying to find out about the coins.

"Look fellows, here is something about the S.S. Republic which sank in 1865 and had a cargo consisting of the type of gold coins we found. It was sunk by a hurricane off the coast of Georgia. The ship's log indicated that another unknown Confederate vessel was traveling with it and was never heard from again. I bet it was the Mudhen."

"Could be. There were a lot of vessels lost during the 1800's. We were very lucky to find that box. Wonder how much is left?" Jake questioned.

"Could we make another dive in the morning?' Jeannie asked excitedly.

"What time is your plane?"

"We are to fly out of Wilmington at four p.m." John answered.

"If the weather is fit in the morning we could go try again. Do not know what this storm is going to do. Usually we have pretty calm water after a big storm like this. We can just wait and see."

Jeannie was beside herself with excitement. She forced herself to eat some lunch after she pulled away form the computer. The rest of the afternoon was spent with Jake and Jeannie running around in the rain to get their tanks refilled and get their gear ready for another dive on Sunday.

After supper, John and Jake had a chance to talk while Jeannie was engrossed in reading the book on shipwrecks and looking up things on the computer. Every now and then she would interrupt Jake and John and give them some information about what she was finding. Occasionally Jake and John would hear the jingling of coins as Jeannie ran her hands through the gold and copper coins and they would smile at each other because of her excitement.

After everyone had gone to bed, Jake was straightening up the kitchen when Jeannie came back out to get a glass of water wearing a very thin white robe. Even though it was a robe it did not leave much to Jake's imagination. She told Jake how much she had enjoyed the day and was looking forward to the dive tomorrow. Before leaving, she went over and gave Jake a big hug and a kiss on the cheek and thanked him again for such a good time.

Before going into her room she stopped and came back and said, "Jake, I just can't sleep. Would you want to go sit on the porch and talk for a while?"

"Sure, it is nice out there since the storm stopped."

A gentle breeze blowing off the ocean kept the mosquitoes and gnats away, and with no moon the sky was ablaze with stars. They just sat there for a few minutes taking in what makes the beach so enjoyable, the tranquility.

"I certainly see why you like it down here. I could really enjoy a lot of this type of relaxation."

"It is nice, but I also like the mountains. It is nice to enjoy the best of both worlds, but I have been so busy with things that I have not had a chance to really enjoy it. I hope that changes soon."

It was quiet for a moment and then Jeannie asked, "I saw your Christian Science books on the shelf in my room and I wondered how you got interested in this religion?"

"Well, my mom was a Scientists and my dad practiced it, but never felt like he wanted to join the church. I have been away from it for a while, but am getting back down to studying again. The closest churches are in Myrtle Beach and Wilmington so it is about an hour's drive if I want to attend a service. Are you familiar with Christian Science?"

"I studied it in college in comparative religion class and know that it is based on a complete trust in God. It was started by Mary Baker Eddy who became a very successful healer. From my reading I know that it takes a lot of study and commitment to get to the point of true spirituality and I admire you for trying to do that."

"It does become your life and it has been such a help to me since Jackie's passing that I know it is where I need to be."

They talked a while longer about religion and then the subject changed to the next day's dive and then to their careers with the FBI, but before long, they both realized that they had to get some sleep.

CHAPTER 29

THE FORCES OF NATURE

SUNDAY, JUNE 8, 2003

Jake heard some noise coming from the kitchen and when he poked his head out of the bedroom he saw Jeannie fixing breakfast.

"You are up early." Jake said with his head poking out of the door.

"Well, I just couldn't sleep. Should we wake John?"

"As soon as he smells that bacon and coffee he will be up. He is not going to miss anything. Have you looked outside? The ocean is like a millpond, not a wave to be seen. That should make for an easier trip out to the dive site. I will be out in just a minute to help you."

By the time Jake made an appearance again, John was up and helping to set the table.

"I cooked some oatmeal. Hope that is all right."

"How did you know that it was my usual Sunday morning breakfast?"

"I didn't, but it is a stick to the ribs kind of food and it should help us on our dive."

Breakfast was dispensed with rather quickly and in a few minutes Jake and Jeannie had their wetsuits on and were headed downstairs. John helped them drag the rubber raft out to the surf. There was a procession of people headed to a beachside church service and several curious people asked them where they were going.

"Just going to do a little ocean sight seeing," Jake said with a smile on his face.

With no waves, they had an easy time launching the raft and it was easy paddling with no current and no waves. Jake checked the GPS and put them on the right course and Jeannie started up a chorus of "Row, row, row your boat." Jake chimed in and they enjoyed the short trip out to the dive site. Jake lowered the anchor, they checked each other's gear and over the side they went. The water was amazingly clear after the storm and teaming with fish as usual.

Jeannie swam ahead and Jake enjoyed watching her move so gracefully through the water. As they approached the Mudhen, they noticed that things had changed. The storm had caused the boat to shift and it had covered up the spot where the chest with the coins had been. They both circled the wreck trying to see if they could locate it, but there was nothing there. Jake gestured with his hands, indicating that he was astonished that they could not find anything. They both dug a little in the sand in various spots, but did not turn up anything. As Jake was circling the boat, he glanced out away from it and noticed something brass sticking out of the sand. He uncovered it and found the ship's sextant. He raised it over his head to let Jeannie see it and she gave him a big thumbs up. He was about ready to call it a day when he saw Jeannie digging in the sand and she came up with a spyglass. He was pleased that she also had found a good trophy from their dive. They looked at each other and Jeannie pointed toward the surface, indicating that she was ready to leave. She took several pictures of the wreck and of Jake and then Jake indicated he would like to take some pictures of her. They had a short photo session with Jeannie in various locations around the boat. The best picture was probably the one of her at the stern where she located the nameplate of the boat and was standing pointing at it.

As they were going toward the surface, they saw a large sea turtle calmly swimming above them. That called for more pictures, but the turtle was quickly out of sight.

In the raft, they took a few minutes to view each other's finds and then they began paddling back to the beach. John and Sandy were at the water's edge to greet them on their return. John had been enjoying playing with Sandy by throwing her ball into the surf and watching her retrieve it. She had little trouble since the ocean was so calm.

They didn't show John what they had found, but told him how disappointed they were that the storm had changed the wreck and that they could not locate the coin chest.

The curious beach walkers asked them if they had found anything, but they just said they saw a lot of interesting fish and a large sea turtle. Back at the cottage, Jake and Jeannie showed John the sextant and the spyglass. He was duly impressed with their finds.

Jeannie helped Jake clean up the equipment and put away the raft and then headed upstairs for a shower and to prepare for her trip back to Washington. After a quick lunch of the remaining sandwich spread left over from the day before, Jeannie and John were ready to leave.

"Jake, since I only have carryon luggage and do not want to answer a lot of question about these coins, will you ship them to me later? I will leave you some money for the postage."

"Will be glad to. That is a good idea. They would sure raise a lot of questions at the security check in. Even with your FBI badge it might be hard to explain."

Jake and John exchanged handshakes and hugs as John loaded the luggage into the rental car. Jeannie finished petting Sandy and gave Jake a big hug and a long kiss on the cheek and said, "Thank you for everything. I really enjoyed our dives and our talk on the porch the other night. Let me know what you decide to do with your coins. See you when we catch John Wesley."

"I hope that will be soon," Jake said as he closed the car door.

He and Sandy watched until they were out of sight and then went back into the cottage. Jake picked up some reading material and headed for the porch and Sandy stretched out in the sun at his feet.

Someone coming through the dunes toward his cottage awakened Jake from his catnap.

"Hey there. May I come up?"

"Sure," Jake said as he recognized Erb, whom he had seen at the pier the other day.

"Just wanted to drop by and show you my latest carving. I was working on it on the pier when we talked the other night."

"Sure, I remember. I had seen your work at the state fair last year. You carve such detailed faces."

Erb handed Jake an Indian that he had carved with such delicate features and lifelike lines that it almost looked like a picture. Jake fingered the silky smooth carving, admiring all the talent that went into making such a fine piece.

"You sure do good work. I never seem to be able to get my tools sharp enough to do that kind of fine work."

"It just takes patience and a good stone and a leather strap."

"Will have to get you to show me how sometime."

"Would be glad to. I have to go. My wife is waiting for me to take her to the Christmas Shop at Calabash."

"That's a place where you can spend a lot of time and money."

"I just usually sit on the porch and carve or play with the ring toss game while she enjoys looking at everything. We will have to get together soon."

Sandy managed to get between Erb and the stairs so he would have to give her some attention before he left.

Jake resumed his reading. Before long it was naptime again, but Sandy woke him in time to be fed and walked before Jake ate his supper and retired for the night.

CHAPTER 30

COACH JAKE

SUNDAY, JUNE 8, 2003

Jake and Sandy had enjoyed their week alone at the beach after John and Jeannie had gone back to Washington.

There was not a cloud in the perfectly blue sky and the light cool ocean breeze made for a wonderful day. It was Sunday and Jake had decided not to drive to Myrtle Beach to attend church, but that he would have his own service and had just finished his Bible Lesson for the week. He had cooked scrambled eggs and country ham for breakfast and was trying to quench his thirst with a nice cold glass of freshly squeezed orange juice.

He was enjoying watching the porpoise frolic out beyond the pier and the pelicans diving for their breakfast just past the breakers. Sandy bounded down the stairs as Jake heard a car door slam underneath his house. He knew it must be friends or Sandy would have barked.

Before he could get out of his chair, the chief and his granddaughter came up the stairs.

"Hello, Chief. I almost did not recognize you out of uniform and in a coat and tie."

"We just got back from the early church service, it is more traditional and we like it better. While Suzie fixed lunch, I decided I would come over and talk to you a minute. This is my granddaughter, Grace. She and her family came for the weekend."

"Well I am glad to meet you Grace, and Chief, I am glad you stopped by. Hope it is a social call and not business."

"Well, it is. I like your new window. You will like the tinted glass."

"I was afraid it would ruin the view, but I believe it makes it better. Cuts out so much glare."

While the men talked, Sandy and Grace enjoyed each other's company as they sat on the floor and she petted Sandy.

"Jake, I have a favor to ask. We were wondering if you would be interested in coaching the little league baseball team that we sponsor. The coach we had moved to Virginia and the league starts in a few weeks as soon as school is out for the summer."

"I did not play beyond the little league myself so I do not know how much of a coach I would be."

"Dan would help, but does not want to take it

267

on full time because he never knows what might come up. We just have a small league of four teams and we play a short season. Thought it might fit into your schedule before you go back to the mountains. You would be a good role model for the boys and best of all you don't have a kid on the team. Our last coach's son played on the team and he was not that good, but he played a lot. We have only about 10 to 12 boys on the team and we do want everyone to play."

"It would be fun. I like the kids and even though I do not know a lot about coaching, I do like baseball."

"Sandy would make a great mascot," Grace piped in.

"Then will you do it?" The chief asked with a big smile on his face.

"I reckon so, but if someone you would rather have comes along, you will not hurt my feelings if you fire me."

"Dan will bring you up to speed and will help you get started."

About that time the chief's cell phone rang and he said, "Will be right there."

"Come on Grace, Grandma has lunch on the table. We had better go. Jake, will you join us?"

"Appreciate it Chief, but not today. Sandy and I need a little alone time and anyway we just finished a big breakfast."

"Roger that," the chief said as he and Grace went down the stairs.

"Well Sandy, what have we gotten ourselves into?" Jake said out loud as she stood watching the chief and Grace go down the stairs.

Sandy and Jake spent the rest of the day, reading, sleeping and walking on the beach with Jake having an occasional thought of what he had gotten himself into.

On Monday morning he ran into Dan at the pier when he went to buy a paper.

"Hello Coach," Dan said as he saw him. "Reckon you can keep yourself out of trouble long enough to get through the season?"

"I hope so. It does seem to follow me around, doesn't it"?

"The beach has been a little lively since you moved in," Dan said laughing.

"When do we start?" Jake asked.

"The first practice is on Wednesday. Will that work for you?"

"Sure. What time?"

"About two-thirty when the kids get out of school. We play at the park over on Highway 17. I have all the equipment."

"See you then," Jake said as he picked up his paper and headed for home.

On Wednesday afternoon, Jake arrived early and in a few minutes Dan showed up. The kids began to arrive and Jake introduced himself to each kid as he arrived. When he could, he also met their parents. Some parents dropped the kids off, but a few stayed to observe the practice.

At 2:30 Jake called them all together and told

them that he wanted them all to have a good time and at the same time learn a little more about baseball and to win a few games if they could. He emphasized that all would get to play in every game

"One kid raised his hand and asked, "When do we get our uniforms?'

Jake referred the question to Dan, who said, "We will give them out the week before the first game."

Jake told them to take the field at the position they would like to play and he began to hit a ball to various parts of the field. Without telling them what to do, he got an idea of the skill level of each player as they fielded the balls knocked to them. It became very obvious who had played before and who was just starting out. Dan gave him a commentary on each boy and what experience he had had as he caught the balls thrown back in for Jake.

After about an hour, Jake called them in and told them that was all for today and that he would see them at the same time the next day.

The next day when the kids showed up, Jake sent them to the field, but this time they took turns at bat and again it was obvious who the good players were, but Jake saw the potential in each kid and hollered encouragement and gave advice to them all at various times during the practice.

At the end of practice he said to Dan, "Did you see the car that came in and circled around and stopped to talk to the drivers of different cars and then left? Can you run this plate for me and see who it is?"

"Probably just some teenagers riding around on their parents' gas. Why are you so interested?"

"I reckon I am overly suspicious, but it looks like it could be drug dealing to me. I see them exchanging something. Here is the number: VRC-6709."

"I will check it out and let you know tomorrow," Dan said as he collected the equipment and put it into the duffel bag.

The next day as Jake entered the park, he saw the same black sedan leaving at the far end of the field. When Dan arrived, Jake said, "He was back again today, but left when I came. What did you find out?"

"The car is registered to Daniel Jacobs. A twenty-five year old male with some minor arrests, but nothing serious. He dropped out of school and at the present time is not working."

"Let's keep an eye out and see if this continues. I saw him talking to one of the parents yesterday. I don't want to do anything to upset the kids."

During the practice Jake and Dan kept an eye out and saw the car come and go several times and stop and talk with several other cars that were coming and going in the park. Jake saw him talking to one of the parents as he got out of his car to watch his son finish practice.

After Jake gave the kids their day-ending pep talk and Dan collected the equipment and left, Jake walked over to where the father was waiting for his son.

"Mr. Presler, I am Jake Johnson, Sam's coach. Could I have a minute of your time in private please?"

"Sure Coach, my son seems to enjoy your style of coaching. He really likes baseball."

"Sam is a good player and will be a real asset to the team, but there is something else I want to talk to you about. I am not a policeman, but I am a former FBI agent and have noticed that you were speaking to Mr. Jacobs as you came up. I am concerned that he might be dealing drugs, but do not want to involve the police until I have a little more information. I am not trying to get you into trouble or interfere in your private life, but I would just like some information."

"Yeah, I kind of know who he is. Now that I have a family, I am not into anything like that, but when I was younger I did smoke a little pot and that is how I know Daniel. When I talked to him today he asked me if I needed anything. I am sure he meant drugs, but we did not talk about it specifically. I don't want to get into any trouble."

"I certainly am not trying to get you into any trouble, but I wanted to get a little more information before I said anything to anyone about what is going on. Your name will never be mentioned again and I waited 'til Mr. Jacobs was gone before I said anything to you. Thanks for your help and be sure to come to the games. It will mean a lot to Sam for you to be here."

"I look forward to it," he said as he shook Jake's hand.

When Jake left the ball field, he went to the police station to talk to the chief and Dan about what he thought was going on.

"Chief, I want to thank you for getting me involved with the kids. I am having a great time and the team is progressing very well."

"Yeah. Dan tells me that it is really going great. They all like you and you are helping them hone their skills. We will be looking for another trophy to go on the shelf."

"Don't know about that yet. We have not seen our competition yet, but we have a practice game on Monday. That should let us know how our guys are coming along. We have some really good players, but I need to talk to you about something else."

"Dan tells me that you think some drug deals are going down in the park."

"There is a lot of activity going on with cars coming and going and all having contact with this fellow Daniel Jacobs. He approached one of the dads today and asked if he could get him anything. Drugs were not mentioned, but the father was sure that was what was meant."

"Just picking up Jacobs will not do us much good. We need to get to the person who is supplying him."

"Yes, I know. Can you get his phone tapped and put him under surveillance?"

"I think I can get a judge to OK that. We certainly do not want the drugs in this county. We need to nip it in the bud."

"I am going to be taking some pictures of the ball team tomorrow and I will try to get some pictures of him and his contacts without him knowing I am getting them."

"That would be great and would help convince the judge that we should be gathering some more information on what he is doing. I will talk to the sheriff about it also since the park is in the county, even though Jacobs lives at Ocean Isle."

When he left the police station Jake drove by the apartment building where Jacobs lived. He noted that it was a pretty fancy place for a fellow who was not working. He did not see the black sedan anywhere and wondered where he might be. He took down the telephone number from the outdoor sign about the apartment, thinking that he might try to get some more information about Mr. Jacobs. The detective in him would not let him leave something like this alone even thought he knew he should leave it up to the authorities.

As he was leaving the area he noticed a pair of tennis shoes strung over a telephone wire and wondered if there was any truth in the rumor that this indicated a place where you could buy drugs.

The next day at practice he was taking pictures of the team in action while Dan put them through their workout. He had two cameras and one had a telephoto lens. He positioned himself so he could shoot the parking lot while looking like he was taking pictures of his team. True to form, he saw the black sedan pull into the parking lot and he began taking pictures. During the next hour, Jake was able to get shots of four different contacts that Jacobs had with different cars that came into the park. He was able to get shots of the license plates of three of the cars so they could find out who he was selling to. His last shots were of some high school girls going to the tennis courts after they stopped and had an exchange with Jacobs. All this was enough to convince Jake that the problem was bigger than he thought.

After practice, he went back to the police station and showed the photos to the chief and Dan. Dan downloaded them into the police computer so that they could use them to convince the Judge to give them a warrant to bug Jacobs' apartment. It would also give them a chance to get some information on the people he was selling to.

While they were talking the county sheriff came into the office.

"Hear you wanted to talk to me, Chief."

"I sure do. Sheriff Connors, this is Jake Johnson, and you know Dan."

"Sure I know Dan, and Jake, it is good to meet you. I have heard a lot about you. Seems like the bad guys just follow you around," The sheriff said as he extended his hand to Jake.

"Glad to meet you, Sheriff. Some of my friends tell me I am a trouble magnet, but I hope not. I also understand that the baseball team your department sponsors is the one to beat this year."

"Well, I hope that is right, but it remains to be seen," the sheriff said with a big smile on his face. The chief and I have a little side bet and I do enjoy the meals he has had to provide in the past, but in reality we are about even. I know you did not call me to talk about baseball. What did you have on your mind, Chief?"

"Well, Jake here, while coaching our little league baseball team, has noticed some unusual activity at the park and he thinks that there is a fellow selling drugs in that area."

"Are you talking about Jacobs?" the sheriff asked.

"Yes."

"We have started keeping an eye on him because we had heard he was dealing. We would like to find his supplier and try to dry that up."

"We were just looking at some photos Jake made today and we wanted to work with you on catching these people."

Dan displayed the photos on the computer and when they were finished, the sheriff said, "Good work, Jake. They sure look like there are deals going down there in the park. I am sorry to see the high school girls involved. I know some of their parents. Do you have a plan, Chief?"

"We want to get a warrant so that we can bug his apartment and tap his phone to find out who his supplier is. Then we will set up the park so we can catch him in the act of dealing and also apprehend some of the people to whom he is selling. Can you help with some manpower to pick up the people as they leave the park? We probably can cut them a deal if they will testify against him and hopefully he will testify against his supplier."

"Sounds like you have a plan. When do you plan to put it into effect?"

"We are working on the warrant and will set up the surveillance as soon as we get the warrant, hopefully tomorrow. We don't want to be in any rush because we want to make a case as far up the line as we can."

The door opened and Dorothy said to the chief, "Judge Samuels is on the phone about the warrant."

"Thanks Dorothy, I will take it in here."

"Hello, Judge," the chief said as he picked up the phone.

Jake, Dan and the sheriff listened to the one-sided telephone conversation and concluded that the Judge had given his approval for the surveillance to be set up and that it could start immediately.

"Thank you judge, we will keep you informed," the chief said as he hung up the telephone.

"It's a go. Dan, call the lab boys and get the phone tapped and the apartment bugged as soon as possible. Sheriff, can you put a plainclothes tail on Jacobs so we will know when we can get into his apartment?"

"Will take care of that right away. We will be in touch," the sheriff said as he got up to leave.

"Jake, we certainly thank you for bringing this to our attention. I am going o give you one of our cell phones that is tied into our system so you can keep us informed on what is going on in the park. Keep taking the pictures of the meetings and let us know which cars to pick up when they leave the park. We want to get several of the buyers after they leave the park before we pick up Jacobs. We need to tie him to a dealer to make this worthwhile."

As Jake got up to leave, Sandy got out from under the table where she had been sleeping and they went out the door. Back at the cottage, Jake plopped down in front of the TV to catch the evening news before he fixed supper.

The next day Jake checked in with the chief before he left for baseball practice. The chief had all his officers in place and they were ready to start their crackdown on this drug traffic ring.

At the park, Jake started practice as the kids showed up. He had them catching fly balls and this gave him a chance to keep an eye out on what else was happening in the park without being obvious. It was not long until he saw the dark sedan enter the park and slowly drive through the parking lot.

It stopped beside a red convertible with a couple of girls in it and Jake was able to snap a picture. Jake got on the phone and reported this to the chief.

The black sedan parked in the parking lot near the tennis court and watched a couple just hitting the ball back and forth. In a few minutes he left the park, but after about forty-five minutes he was back. He parked in front of the restrooms and when he was inside Jake saw one of the maintenance men walk by the sedan and place something under the wheel well and then go back to his work. In a few minutes, Jacobs came out of the restroom and drove to the other end of the park where he stopped and chatted with someone in a black pickup truck. It was too far away for Jake to get a picture, but he relayed a description of the truck to the chief before it left the park.

Jake got busy with his team and missed a couple of other transactions. The parents started coming to pick up their kids and Jake got his equipment together and prepared to leave the park. Jacobs had just left the park ahead of Jake and when Jake realized that he was behind Jacobs, Jake called the chief and told him he was going to tail Jacobs. The chief reminded him to stay clear so that he would not spook Jacobs. When Jake realized that Jacobs was going back to his apartment, he cut off and left this detective work to the police and sheriff's department.

He stopped at the police station before going home and found the chief talking to the man in the pickup truck that Jake had reported.

"Hello. Jake," the chief said as he entered the door. "This is Peter Wiley who I have just convinced to help us build our case against Jacobs."

Jake shook Mr. Wiley's hand and said, "Thank you. You are doing a good thing."

"I was not buying, Jacobs was just trying to

sell to me," Wiley said to try to convince Jake and the chief that he was really not involved.

"He is getting brazen if he is soliciting in the park rather than just meeting his clients there. If we can just find his supplier we will be all set."

"Our surveillance is in place and we should have a lead on that person shortly," the chief replied.

The chief's cell phone rang and he stepped into another room to take the call. Coming back into the room, the chief said to Jake, "We have Jacobs staked out at a house that we believe is his supplier's. Do you want to come?"

"Sure. I would not want to miss this for the world. I want these men off the street."

"Thank you for your help, Mr. Wiley. We will be back in touch if we need you. Please do not say anything to anyone about this."

Two sheriff's deputies and Dan were already in place at the house and the sheriff arrived just a minute later.

"Dan, you and the two deputies go to the back and we will call on Mr. Jacobs and his friend. Be careful. We do not know if they are armed or not. Jake, put on this vest. I do not want anything to happen to you before baseball season is over," the chief said, laughing.

Just as the chief was about to knock on the door, it opened. When Jacobs saw who it was, he slammed the door, but the chief had it open before he could lock it. The chief and the sheriff went in with drawn guns and heard running footsteps and then the back door opening.

"Stay right where you are," Dan yelled at the two men trying to flee the house out the back door.

The deputies put the two men in handcuffs, and read them their rights, and took them to the patrol car.

"Put them in separate cars," The chief yelled to Dan as they took them around the house to where the cars were parked.

Inside the house, Jake had a chance to look around. "Looks like we caught them with the goods," Jake said as the chief and sheriff re-entered the house.

"There's a lot of different drugs and a lot of cash. They did not have time to hide anything."

"Dan, get some pictures and then you and the deputy search the house completely and catalogue everything you find. See if you can find anything that will tell us who this fellow is buying his drugs from."

"This fellow's name is Rick Matthews and according to his computer he has been having a lot of conversations with a Rachel Erikson who lives at Little River. She is connected with the gambling boats. She could either be another buyer or his supplier. Either way, the gambling boats would be a good way to smuggle the drugs into the country or to sell them to the gambling customers or both," Dan explained to the group in the house.

"We will have the lab boys go through the computer to see what else they can find," the chief said to the sheriff.

The chief wrapped up his work at the house and said to Jake, " You ready to leave?"

"Yes, I am glad it went without a hitch and that we at least got these two off the streets if it does not go any higher."

"Oh, I think we will get at least one more layer before we quit. One of these two will rat his dealer out."

Back at the station, the chief again thanked Jake for his work on the case and they chatted about the baseball team for a few minutes before Jake left the station for his house.

During the next few weeks, Jake continued to hold practice and then they started their games. The team responded well to Jake's coaching and won most of their games. The chief kept Jake apprised of the developments in the drug case. They were able to arrest Mrs. Erikson and then the feds took over and went one step higher in the chain and also took Jim Combs from Myrtle Beach out of the picture.

As the baseball season came to an end with Jake's team winning the championship, Jake got restless for the mountains and planned to return to his Weaverville cabin for a while. During the next few months Jake alternated between the seashore and the mountains, depending on whether or not he had a rental at the beach cottage.

CHAPTER 31

BACK IN THE MOUNTAINS

TUESDAY, SEPTEMBER 30, 2003

An unexpected early snowfall was dusting the ground with heavy snowflakes as Jake drove up to the cabin. Sandy was restless and could not wait to get out of the truck. She bounded out of the truck as Jake opened the door and scurried around sniffing and making her marks as she surveyed the whole scene. She spooked a doe and her fawn out of the front yard as she made her rounds of the house.

Jake unlocked the house, turned up the heat and returned to the truck to get the rest of his things, including some groceries he had picked up on the way in. Everything in the house looked fine except that it had a light covering of dust since he had not been there in a while. Need to get someone to keep up the place when I am not here, he thought.

Sandy scratched at the door and Jake let her in. He had just finished filling her water bowl and putting out her food which she quickly devoured. She then made her rounds in the cabin checking out everything.

The cell phone rang and he saw on the phone screen that it was Barbara.

"Guess where I am," he said as he answered the phone.

"You must be in the mountains." She replied, laughing.

"Just got here a few minutes ago. Everything is fine, but there was no one to greet me and to have turned up my heat. Where were you?" Jake said, poking fun at her.

"I would love to be back in the mountains. This city life is not what it is cracked up to be. Of course I have not been here very much lately. Malcolm has had me going all over the place. Still no word on John Wesley. It is as if he has just dropped off the earth."

"That would be a great working out," Jake said with enthusiasm.

"Saw Jeannie the other day and she was still excited about her trip to the coast with you and John. I need to be careful letting her spend too much time with you. She is a beautiful girl."

"Way too young for me and anyway you were supposed to be there instead of her," Jake replied, hoping to change the subject.

"Have a call coming in. Have to get it. Talk to you later," Barbara said as she clicked off the phone and Jake was left standing there with no one to talk to.

Jake heard his alarm go off and saw a car coming up his driveway, which he recognized as the sheriff's car. He went to the door as Ken got out. Sandy bounded out of the door and went to meet Ken like a long lost friend. Ken stopped and petted her, showing that he was glad to see her also.

"Hello there, Jake. I was out on patrol and saw the truck in your drive and came up to be sure it was you. Good to have you back in the mountains. We haven't had any excitement since you left," Ken said jokingly.

"Glad to be back. The coast is nice, but it is always good to be up here. Thanks for checking up on things for me."

"Still no word on what has happened to John Wesley. Since you are back, maybe he will show up again."

"I hope so. I am tired of looking over my shoulder. Come in and have a cup of coffee."

"I had better save that for later. I need to get back to the office. There is a man out today and that is why I am out on patrol. We will catch up later."

"Tell your wife hello for me. See you later."

Jake and Sandy stood at the door and watched Ken drive away. He certainly has been a good friend, Jake thought. In a few minutes he and

Sandy got in the truck and went to the post office to pick up his mail. He missed having Barbara around to do things like that for him, but he also missed her good company. The mountains were just not the same without her being there. He went through his mail, but found nothing of any importance as usual. As he sat and watched the bird feeders out his big window, he regained his sense of contentment. The doe and fawn that Sandy had scared off returned to munch on his green grass and his bushes. They were beautiful and he enjoyed watching them. Sandy came over for a pat on the head and lay down beside the chair and stared out the window with Jake.

When Jake awoke the next morning, the ground was covered with about an inch of snow. He got up, dressed, ate and fed Sandy, and decided he would go on a hike up the log slide to take some pictures of the early fall snow. Sandy was anxious as Jake got his equipment together. She bounded out the door and raced around the house to see if she could chase a deer, but there were none available at this time.

Jake stopped many times to take pictures of various objects made beautiful by the sun on the snow. When he reached the top of the log slide, the vistas were magnificent. It looked like a fairyland. He knew that Barbara would have loved to paint some of these scenes and Jackie would have been spellbound by these beautiful scenes of nature. He missed both of these people and was feeling pretty sad when in front of him a beautiful buck deer emerged into a clearing and in a few minutes two does followed. Jake reached down and got Sandy by the collar, snapped on her leash so she would not ruin this beautiful scene by bounding after them. Jake got several very good shots before Sandy could not contain herself and started barking and the three deer were immediately gone. Continuing on the trail, Jake was startled as he flushed out two ruffled grouse which were gone before he could get a picture. On the side of the cliff, he sat on a rock and watched two hawks soar in the distance. He was transfixed by the beauty of the moment as the rising sun changed the landscape minute by minute. He sat for a long time looking and taking pictures.

On his way back to the cabin, he went by Reams Creek and absorbed the beauty of the snow and rocks and churning water. It was a wonderland, but it was beginning to go away as the sun quickly melted the light snow. He did have the best of both worlds: the beautiful mountains with their changing seasons and the magnificent ocean that gave a sense of what eternity must be like.

Back at the cabin he enjoyed sitting in front of a roaring fire and just relaxing, something he did not seem to do a lot of. For the next few months he and Sandy enjoyed their solitude and an occasional visit from Ken.

He began to get restless and decided he wanted to be back at the coast again. He packed and the next day he and Sandy were on the road again.

CHAPTER 32

JOHN WESLEY WILLIAMS AGAIN

FRIDAY, OCTOBER 3, 2003

Jake thought he was going to be able to make it to the cottage, but he was in bad need of a rest stop, so he pulled into the rest area on Highway 17 just outside of Shallotte. He was getting into his truck when a car pulled up beside him and when the man got out of the car, he did a double take. There was John Wesley.

He tried to call the police, but his cell phone battery was dead. As John Wesley emerged from the building, for some reason Jake decided to follow him and see where he was going. He managed to get his cell phone plugged into the charger and ducked down so he would not be recognized.

Jake could see him get into his car and take out his cell phone and dial a number. In a second, surprisingly, Jake's cell phone rang.

288

"Yes. This is Jake," he said in a low voice.

"This is John Wesley Williams. We need to talk."

"What about"

"I want to make a deal with you."

"What about? The last time I saw you you were trying to kill me."

"I have had a change of heart. I know that I am not going to be able to get my money back from you and the fellow who hired me has reneged on another deal and I want to get even with him. I am ready to give him up if you will help me disappear. I am tired of running. I know it does not matter to you, but your wife's death was an accident. I did not mean to shoot her. That was never in the plan."

"You are right, Accident or not she is still gone. I would like to get the person who put you up to this, but I am not sure I can just let you go."

"Well, I recently found out that I have just a few months to live and I would like to try to make it right with you."

"How do I know that you are not just lying to me to get me in a position to finish the job?"

"I can give you my doctor's name in Vegas and he will verify my diagnosis. If you want this fellow you had better decide to take this deal because time is running out."

"Where are you?"

"I am in the beach area."

"How can I contact you?"

"Here is my phone number: 767-438-3426. Call me by nine in the morning. If you tell anyone about this the deal is off," John Wesley said as he hung up his phone.

Jake watched as John Wesley pulled out of the parking area and headed north on Highway 17. Jake let a few cars get between them and then he followed him. John Wesley pulled into the Holiday Inn parking lot and went inside. In a few minutes he came out and, moved his car, and took his bag inside. Jake moved his truck until he could see the building clearly. In a few minutes he saw someone standing at the open window in the second floor corner room. The best he could tell it looked like John Wesley.

Jake could not decide what to do. He had a gut feeling that the offer was for real. He left the parking lot with his head reeling, trying to think what he should do. He drove to his cottage and unloaded his stuff and took care of Sandy. He plopped down in his recliner and tried to weigh all the options in his head. He felt that John Wesley was sincere about Jackie and knew that nothing he did to him would bring Jackie back, but might complicate his life. The person who triggered this whole horrid experience was still out there and Jake would like to have him brought to justice. The part of the deal about letting John Wesley go free was still giving him some trouble, but he knew that deals were made all the time to get to a higher player and if John Wesley really was dying what could be the harm?

He thought about calling John or Barbara, but

what could they tell him except that he must not let John Wesley get away? He had to make his own decision and keep it to himself. He needed to get information from John Wesley that would hold up in court, devise a plan to fake John Wesley's death, and then help him get away.

He decided to call a lawyer friend in Washington who could help him get the information about the third party that would hold up in court. He picked up the phone and dialed Bob Seawell's number.

A receptionist answered the phone, "Schwentker and Seawell, how may I direct your call?"

"Bob Seawell, please. This is Jake Johnson calling."

"Well hello, Jake. It has been a long time. How are you? Have not heard from you since you moved to the mountains of North Carolina."

"I am doing fine. Bob, I need your help. I need you to come to North Carolina for a day to take a deposition from a fellow who has some information that I need to be sure will hold up in court. I don't know anyone down here who I can trust and I know that if you do it, it will be done right and it needs to be done in the next couple of days or I will lose my information."

"Let me look at my calendar. Where would I be going?"

"To Wilmington, North Carolina. We could take care of it at the airport and you could catch the next flight back to Washington. I will bring the person, a laptop and a notary and we can find a quiet place at the airport that we can use."

"Do you want to give me any more details at this time?"

"I had rather not do it over the phone."

"OK. Give me a few minutes to get a flight and I will call you right back. I know you would not be calling for this if it were not urgent."

"Thanks, Bob. I will owe you big time."

Jake hung up the phone and relaxed in his chair, relieved that he had taken this step and felt like it was the thing to do. All he had to do now was to find a way to make John Wesley disappear so the authorities would stop looking for him and he could pass on in peace.

In a few minutes the phone rang and Jake answered, "This is Jake."

"Jake, I have a flight that will arrive in Wilmington at 10 a.m. with a returning flight that leaves at twelve noon. Are you sure that will give us enough time?"

"I certainly think so. It will be a short document and I am sure we can take care of it in that time frame. I will meet you at the gate. Do I need to bring anything?"

"Just your man. Meet me at the public computer room so you do not have to bother going through security. We can type it out on my computer and all the airports now have office work areas where we can make some hard copies. We can get an airport official to witness the document and I am a notary so you do not need to involve anyone else. It seems that you want to keep this as simple as possible and not involve any more people than you have to."

"You are right. We will meet you at the airport. Thanks again for being willing to do this."

"You and Jackie were always good friends and I miss seeing you. See you in the morning."

Jake hung up the phone and then dialed John Wesley's number.

"This is Jake. I have worked it out with a lawyer friend and we are to meet him at the Wilmington airport at 10 a.m. He does not know any of the details as to what this is about. Do you want to ride with me or come alone?"

"I will come alone. Not that I do not trust you, but I want to keep my options open."

"Meet us at the public computer room at 10 A.M."

"I will be there."

Jake hung up the phone feeling pretty good that it had worked out this well so far. He hoped John Wesley would hold up his end of the bargain.

It was hard for Jake to sleep. He kept mulling the whole situation over and over in his mind. He wanted to be sure he was doing the right thing. He wished he had someone to talk to about it, but knew that in the end it must be his decision and his only. The reality was that he could not tell anyone about what he was going to do. Helping a known felon to escape from the authorities was no small deal. He could be in real trouble.

When the bright sun appeared in his window, Jake was already awake. He had been so fretful in his sleep that Sandy had slept by his bed.

He lay there for a few more minutes thinking about how the day was going to play out and then he bounded out of bed and prepared for his trip to Wilmington.

Sandy was not pleased that she was being left alone and stared after Jake as he went down the stairs. She whined a little, but Jake stopped and said, "It's alright girl. I will be back in a little while."

The drive to the Wilmington airport was uneventful. Jake arrive at 9:45 and made his way to the public computer room then and staked out a small private office where they could meet and transact their business. He drew the blinds and went out into the public area to wait for Bob and John Wesley. He felt better because he had already spotted John Wesley seated where he could watch the room without being seen and surmised that he was going to wait until Bob and Jake were both there and he had checked out the area to be sure that there were no cops around.

Jake heard them announce the arrival of Flight 234 from Washington and in a few minutes he saw Bob coming his way. Jake met him outside the room where John Wesley could see them.

"Good morning, Bob. Thank you for coming," Jake said as he shook hands with Bob.

"Is our man here yet?" Bob asked.

"He is in the building and I think he will be

here in a few minutes," Jake answered.

Just as Jake was about to start telling Bob the whole story, John Wesley entered the room. Jake introduced him to Bob and they shook hands.

"Let's sit down and talk this thing through," Jake said motioning both men to a seat at the table.

"Bob, here is our situation. John Wesley, you stop me if I say something that is not right. John Wesley was hired by someone to kill me and in the process he accidentally shot Jackie. At the trial he would not give up the name of the person who hired him. I am now convinced that shooting Jackie was an accident and that he did not really mean to shoot her. He was convicted in court of the murder and was sentenced to prison, but escaped when the bus that was transporting him to prison had an accident. He now has a terminal illness and says he will tell us the name of the person who hired him to kill me. He has some documentation he says will prove that this man hired him. I want to be sure that what he has will hold up in court if he is not around to testify."

John Wesley interrupted and said, "I do not plan to be around to go through any trial. Part of my deal is that I will disappear and the authorities will not know where I am. I want to live what is left of my life in peace and not end up in jail again. If we cannot work that out, then there is no deal and the person who hired me will never be punished."

"What you and Jake work out as far as your disappearance is up to the two of you. As an officer of the court, I do not want to know anything about that. When I hear what information you have and get your sworn testimony, I can advise the two of you if I think it will hold up in court to convict Mr. X of contracting to have Jake killed," Bob said to them.

"I think that John Wesley and I can come up with a way to make him disappear without involving anyone else. Not sure what will happen to me if I do this and the authorities find out about it, but I am willing to take that chance," Jake said.

"Well, if we want to do this then let's hear what John Wesley has to say. Will you let me tape this conversation?" Bob asked John Wesley.

"Yes, if it will help you may tape it."

"I can type up your statement from the tape and that way I will be sure I have what you want to say. Go ahead when you are ready."

"I am John Wesley Williams and I am making this statement without any pressure from anyone. I have contacted lawyer Seawell and he has met me in Wilmington, N. C. and we are in the Wilmington airport. Doctor Britt has told me that I just have a short time to live. I was convicted of the murder of Jackie Johnson in 2002, but at that time I would not give the court the name of the person who hired me to kill Jake Johnson. The killing of Jackie was an accident. I did not mean to shoot her at the Quick Market, but the bullet went astray and she was shot and I am very sorry about that.

John Billings from Las Vegas, Nevada was the man who hired me to kill Jake Johnson. At the time, I was dating his daughter and he had let his daughter go to prison for a crime he committed. John Billings shot one of the men who worked for him because he stole some money from him. The father blamed Jake Johnson for his daughter being caught and going to prison. He offered me $600,000 to kill Jake. I made two attempts to kill Jake, but was not successful. In the meantime, while in prison, Kathy Billings was killed by one of the inmates when they got into a fight. I later learned that her father had hired that inmate to kill her because Kathy had gotten mad with her father and was ready to testify against him. Her father had paid me more money to keep quiet about the whole thing. Here are some pictures of me with John Billings and a taped telephone conversation of him talking to me about what I should do. There is also a second conversation about me loosing the money when lightning hit the airplane. He offered me $800,000 if I would try again and keep quiet about the whole matter. He convinced me I could get my money back from Jake, which I was never able to do and Billings only paid me $400,000 of the $800,000 that he owed me. That is when I found out about him having his daughter killed and decided that I might be next. I decided to come clean with Jake because I really felt bad about accidentally killing his wife. It was during that time that I got the report from the doctor."

Bob stopped the tape and said, "John Billings is a real piece of work. Not sure the courts will let us use the tapes, but they give us a time frame and we can use his telephone records to help verify this. The photographs put the two of you together and if we could get the inmate who killed his daughter to talk, we could make a pretty good case against him. What is the inmate's name?"

Bob turned the recorder back on and John Wesley said, "The inmate who killed Kathy is Jes Simmons and he is in the federal pen in Nevada. He never got anything from John Billings and is pretty sore at him, but is afraid to say anything because of all the connections John Billings has in the prison."

"Do you have any other information that would be of use in trying to convict Mr. Billings?"

"The man that Billings shot was Sam Purdee. I was there when he shot him and I can tell you where his body was hidden."

"If we cannot get him for hiring you to kill Jake maybe the authorities can convict him of that murder. What can you tell us about that?"

"It was March 1998 and Billings was building a new club in Vegas called the Cat House and they were paving the parking lot. We buried the body in the southwest corner of the rear parking lot where the dumpster sits. The gun that had Billings' prints on it was also thrown into the grave."

"Did you have anything to do with the actual murder?"

"No. I was in the office after midnight when Billings and Purdee got into an argument about missing money and Billings shot him twice and then we took the body out the back door and dug the grave where they were going to pour concrete the next day. Sam Carson was the paving contractor and he was Billings' brother-in-law so he probably knew about the body because they got that part covered first thing the next morning.

Purdee was a single man with no family, so there was not much done about his disappearance. That is about all I know."

"Well Jake, I think we have enough that Billings will definitely go to jail if John is telling us the truth."

"I am telling you the truth. It happened just as I told you."

"I have no reason not to believe you. Bob, do we need any more from John Wesley?" Jake asked.

"No I just need to type this up and get John Wesley to sign it. Jake, I think you should disappear for a few minutes while we wrap this up. Don't think it is wise for you and John Wesley to be seen together. When I have this typed up, I will go find us an airport official to witness the signature. Give me about thirty minutes and I will have it ready."

"No cops," John Wesley said emphatically.

"You can get someone from the airport office," Jake said.

Jake left the room as Bob had suggested and Bob and John Wesley proceed to put the document together. Bob left and returned in a few minutes with Mrs. Talbort, a receptionist in the airport office.

"I am John's attorney and we thank you for

helping us out with this document. We just need to have you witness it being signed and sign the document as a witness. Please fill in the contact information in case it ever has to be verified that this man signed the document. You are just saying that you witnessed him signing the document, not what is in the document."

John Wesley signed the document and the copies and Mrs. Talbort signed as a witness after Bob notarized the copies.

"Normally a witness is not required, but this is a sensitive issue and I want to be able to prove that this man signed this document. As an added aid do you mind if we get a picture of the three of us holding the document," Bob asked Mrs. Talbort.

Bob stepped out in the hall and asked a passer by if he would take a picture for him. Bob explained how the camera worked and the man got a couple of shots of the three of them with the document.

When the picture-taking was done, Bob tried to pay Mrs. Talbort for her time, but she said no, that it was part of her job at the airport. Bob and John both thanked her profusely as Bob opened the office door for her.

Jake had been watching from a distance and when he saw Mrs. Talbort leave, he returned to the room.

"Well, that wraps it up for me. Do you want to get a bite to eat before my plane leaves for Washington?" Bob asked Jake and John Wesley.

"Not me. I don't want some rookie cop who memorizes all the mug shots to recognize me. I need to get out of this public place as fast as I can," John Wesley said very quickly and headed for the door.

"Let me speak to you just for a moment," Jake said directly to John Wesley.

"Bob, I hope this gets that S.O.B in jail in a hurry," John said to Bob.

"Well, it should, but it will take a little time to build the case. Thank you for your part. I know Jake appreciates it."

Jake walked out with John Wesley and asked, "Are you ready to go tonight?"

"Yes. My friend will pick me up at the Ocean Isle Airport about two in the morning."

"I have a plan that will make it look like you committed suicide. Bring an old shoe, a shirt and pants, your wallet and your cell phone along with your car to the airport tonight and I will explain it all to you then. Be there about 1:30 so we can have everything set by the time your friend arrives."

John turned and walked away. Jake stood and watched him go and wondered if he would show up that night.

Bob and Jake went to the snack bar and got some lunch. They talked about old times and tried to put the present out of their minds.

Right before it was time for Bob to leave, Jake game him information on how to contact him and said, "Go talk to Malcolm and get the case started as soon as you can. When you lay it all out for them, they will take it and run with it. You probably will not have to be involved anymore. I really appreciate your coming and doing this for me. I want to get this behind me."

"I am sure you do, old friend. I am glad I could help. Come see me when you get back to Washington."

"I will."

Jake walked him to the security gate, shook his hand, gave him a hug and walked away. He was ready to put the next part of the plan into action.

CHAPTER 33

A TALL LEAP

SUNDAY, OCTOBER 5, 2003

Back at his cottage, Jake spent the afternoon and early evening thinking about his plan and preparing for the disappearance of John Wesley Williams. He had to convince the authorities that John Wesley was dead without their having to have the body. He put his wetsuit and a snorkeling mask, and a small digital recorder in a watertight pack and put it in his truck. He put his bicycle in the back of the truck. He fed Sandy, ate his supper, and then took her for a walk. It was about one o'clock when he left his cottage. He observed that the police patrol car was parked in front of the station and there were lights on in the station. He knew that Dan was in the building. He drove his truck to the cabin at the end of Gause Landing and parked it in the driveway. He got his pack and put it on, then got the bicycle and rode back toward the airport. There appeared to be no one up this time of evening. He quickly reached the airport and put his bike behind a hanger to wait for John Wesley, but he did not have to wait. John Wesley was already there and when he saw that it was Jake, he came out of the open hanger so Jake could see that he was there.

"Are you ready?" Jake asked.

"I talked to my friend just a few minutes ago and he is about fifteen minutes away."

"Good. We don't need much time, but I need you to make a recording that I can play over your cell phone to alert the police that you are going to jump off the Sunset Beach Bridge. I have written it out so you can read it into my recorder. Once you are in the air and I am in place, I will call 911 and play the message from your cell phone. I will park your car at the top of the bridge with the door open and when I see the police coming I will wait until they can see me, and then I will jump from the bridge. The tide and current will take me down the waterway where I have my truck parked and I will be back in my cottage in just a few minutes before they have a chance to get their equipment in the water to try and find you. Hopefully that will convince them that you have killed yourself. It would not be unusual for them not to be able to find a body because of the vast amount of water and the strong tides."

"Will you be able to make that jump and be safe?" John asked Jake.

"The military trained me to do such things and I have done it many times."

Jake handed John the note and recorder and after he had had a chance to read it through, Jake said, "Just talk in a natural voice so they can understand what you are saying."

John recorded the message and Jake played it back to be sure it was there. As he was finishing they heard the approaching plane and John and Jake walked toward John's car.

"The shoe and old clothes and wallet are on the front seat and the keys are in the car. Thank you for helping me and I am really sorry that I have caused you so much trouble."

"Well, if you recall, I got paid pretty well for it," Jake said.

The plane taxied toward the hangar and John got a suitcase out of his car, waved at Jake, and walked toward the plane. In a moment they were loaded and taxiing down the runway. Jake watched as the plane lifted off the runway, banked to the right and was on its way. Jake did not know where they were going nor did he care,

Jake put the bicycle in the trunk of the car and headed back to Gause Landing where he put the bike in the back of his truck and headed toward Sunset Beach in John's car. There was no one to be seen anywhere, which pleased Jake. Before going onto the bridge, Jake stopped and put on his wet suit and stuffed his clothes in the watertight pack. While doing this, Jake found a pill bottle from Smith Drugs in Las Vegas with a prescription written by Dr. Britt for Williams. The label said "For Pain". There was one pill left in the bottle. This was a nice addition Jake thought. He drove to the top of the bridge and parked the car with the headlights lighting up the east rail of the bridge. He took out the cell phone and recorder, dialed 911, and when they answered he played this message:

"I'm John Wesley Williams. John Billings is the man that hired me to kill Jake Johnson. I do not have long to live and I want to stop hurting and suffering. I am going to jump off the Sunset Beach Bridge. You will find my car on top of the bridge. I have given lawyer Bob Seawell all the information about John Billings. Please tell Jake Johnson I am sorry for all the trouble I have caused him. I have no family or next of kin."

He left John Wesley's wallet on the seat of the car and put the old shoe on the railing of the bridge. Jake erased the message on the recorder and put the recorder in his pack. He climbed over the rail on the east side of the bridge wearing Williams' old clothes over his wet suit. From the top of the bridge he had a pretty clear view back toward the Sunset Beach Police Department and he watched to see the flashing lights of the patrol car. He wanted to wait until he was sure they could see him on the bridge in the bright headlights of the car. He was not really expecting to see anyone come from the beach side, but there must have been someone on patrol in that area because the flashing of the bright lights and the blaring of the siren were coming up the bridge. The tide was high and running north and the night was dark and Jake could hardly see the water because there was no moon. He let the patrol car get close enough to see him jump, and over the side he went.

The patrol car slid to a stop. The patrolman jumped out and headed for the rail to try to see the person in the water, but his little flashlight would not penetrate the darkness.

The military had trained Jake well and he had no trouble making a very smooth entry into the water. In a moment he popped back to the surface. He slipped out of John Wesley's old pants and shirt, put on his snorkeling gear and started quietly swimming toward Gause Landing. When he looked back, there was a second patrol car on the bridge and both men were standing at the railing, trying to see what was happening in the water. The tide had already swept Jake well away from the bridge and the policemen had no idea where he was.

In a few minutes he heard other sirens and suspected that fire trucks and EMS vehicles would be on the scene in a short time. He eased to the landward side of the channel so he could avoid the strong currents that would be pulling him out the inlet between Ocean Isle and Sunset. He took one of John Wesley's shoes out of his pack and sent it sailing in the strong current at the inlet. The shoe should wash up on shore somewhere along the coast in the next few days. Jake was a strong swimmer and this was really no problem for him. In a few minutes he was pulling himself up onto the dock at Gause Landing. This had gone even better than he had expected. Now if he could just get into his truck and back to his cottage before anyone saw him, he would be fine.

As he walked up the stairs of his cottage, he heard his phone start ringing. When he reached the phone he answered in a very groggy voice, "This is Jake."

"This is Dan. Sorry to wake you, but John Wesley Williams just jumped off the Sunset Beach Bridge. Thought you might be interested."

"How do you know it was him?"

"He called 911 and gave them an interesting message."

"Sandy and I will be right there."

Jake got out of his wetsuit and quickly took a hot shower, and dressed. He and Sandy were out the door in a matter of minutes. He hung his bike on the rack in the storage room and checked his truck for anything else he might have left. When he arrived at the bridge, Chief Prevatte and Dan converged on his truck.

"Well, it looks like some of your troubles might be over," The chief said in a cheerful voice.

"Are you sure it was John Wesley? Jake asked.

"It is his car and his wallet was on the front seat along with a prescription for pain killers. He identified himself to the 911 operator and told her he had a terminal illness and wanted to quit suffering."

"If I had gotten to him, he would have had a terminal illness for sure. How do we know he did not survive the jump and this was all a ploy?" Jake blurted out.

"The rescue boys found his shirt and pants floating in the water and the tide is so strong, he was probably swept out to sea at the inlet."

"Some more potential good news for you. He named the person who hired him to try to kill you."

"Who was that?" Jake asked quickly.

"A fellow by the name of Billings."

"Yeah, I remember him. I put his daughter away for killing a man and she ended up getting killed in prison. So this is what this has all been about. He wanted revenge on me," Jake said angrily.

"We will let the Bureau know all about this first thing in the morning."

Jake noticed Sandy sniffing around the car and the bridge and looking back at him as if to say, you have been here haven't you. Jake smiled to himself and thought, this will be our little secret.

"There's nothing I can do here. I am going back and finish my sleep, if I can. Might sleep with one eye open though because I am not convinced that John Wesley is actually dead."

"We will be in touch in the morning," the chief said as Jake called Sandy and they got back in the truck. So far so good, Jake thought as he reached over and patted Sandy on the head.

It was 3:30 in the morning when he crawled into bed to try to get a little sleep before his phone would start ringing when the news hit the bureau.

CHAPTER 34

MANHUNT OVER

MONDAY, OCTOBER 6, 2003

By 10 o'clock, Jake had had calls from Malcolm, Barbara, John, Ken, and Chief Prevatte. There was not a question in any of their minds that John Wesley Williams was dead and finally gone from the scene and that Jake could relax.

Chief Prevatte had already cleaned out the motel room where John Wesley had stayed and found nothing to indicate anything, but suicide. Malcolm had called Bob Seawell and gotten enough information from him to send his agents to pick up Billings under Barbara's supervision. John had been sent to Vegas to oversee the location of Purdue's body encased in the cement under the dumpster behind Billings' nightclub. The rescue team had searched the waterway and had found nothing, but the shirt and pants of John Wesley. A thorough search of John Wesley's car had not turned up anything of any consequence. His cell phone had been dumped so there were no calls to trace except the 911 call. A couple of days later a shoe matching the one on the bridge washed ashore at Holden's Beach giving credence to the theory that John Wesley had washed out to sea.

Jake and Sandy stayed around the beach for a few days and then drove down to Brookgreen Gardens to take some pictures of the statuary for a national publication. At Murles Inlet Jake found a captain who would let Sandy go out with them and he went on a trip to the Gulf Stream and had moderate luck fishing, but the peace and quiet was what Jake was really after. He had killed a week and then it was back to the beach house.

He was greeted by a ringing telephone when he entered the cottage and the lights were all blinking on his answering machine.

"This is Jake."

"Man, where have you been?" John answered sarcastically.

"Taking some pictures and doing a little fishing. What's up?"

"We uncovered Purdue's body and sure enough there was a gun in the same hole with Billings' fingerprints all over it. He was so sure it would never be found he did not even bother to wipe it down. With the information that lawyer

Seawell has from John Wesley we will be able to put him away for good."

"Sounds good to me. I had rather not get mixed up in it at all if I can help it.
Don't want to stir up another hornet's nest and have to start looking over my shoulder again. Where's Barbara?"

"She has gotten Billings settled in prison and is headed back to Washington. She wondered where you have been. She sounded a little peeved not knowing."

"I just this minute walked in the house. I will give her a call. We will have to find another excuse to get together now that John Wesley is out of the picture. Talk to you later,"

Jake settled back in his recliner and after Sandy had checked everything out, she came and lay at his feet. The view just got better and better every time he looked out on the beautiful ocean.

The weeks rolled by and Jake and Sandy enjoyed the solitude of the coast. Jake got several calls to line up photography work as his reputation spread. He took Susan with him to the egrets' nesting site over near Sunset Beach and she was astonished. She did not know it existed and had never seen so many beautiful large white birds in her life. She hired him on the spot to provide the museum with some photographs.

Barbara stayed so busy they could not work out a time to see each other. Malcolm informed Jake of the date of the trial of Billings. They were prosecuting him for the murder of Purdee, which was fine with Jake. He just wanted to see him in jail. There had been no questions about John Wesley Williams and everyone assumed he was drowned when he jumped off the Sunset Beach Bridge. The FBI paid lawyer Seawell for all his work so Jake got off scott free.

Chief Prevatte called Jake to come to his office. He wanted to see him in person because he needed to tell him something. Jake and Sandy stopped by the police station the next time they were out.

"Good morning, Dan. Is the chief in?" Jake said as he and Sandy entered the office.

"Yes. He is in his office, go on back."

When the chief saw that it was Jake, he got up from his desk and shook his hand and said, "Hello, Jake. Thanks for coming by. I have a little something for you."

He returned to his desk and got an envelope out of his desk drawer and said, "You have been so helpful to the police department that the Town Council wanted to make you a consultant for the police department and to give you this check for the work you have already done."

"That is very nice. I was not expecting anything like that, but I am not one to turn down a check. I was just glad to do it and enjoyed being back in police work for a little while. I hope they do not expect too much because I will be spending a lot of time in the mountains."

"They realize that and just wanted to let you know that you were appreciated and wanted to be able to get your help in the future."

"Please convey my thanks to them," Jake said to the chief as he shook his hand again with a big smile on his face.

"Thank you, Chief, I am sure you had a lot to do with this. I will be seeing you around and will be talking to you later."

CHAPTER 35

PRISON VISIT

TUESDAY, DECEMBER 23, 2003

A month after Billings was tried and sentenced to federal prison, Jake flew out to Kansas to Leavenworth Penitentiary to pay him a visit. Malcolm had made arrangements for Jake to see him. Jake was no stranger to prisons, but it was still a very depressing place. The security measures were very strict so Jake was not concerned that it took him a while to get through all the red tape. He was a little surprised that Billings would agree to see him. He probably was glad to talk to anyone from the outside. As Jake waited in the visiting area, he wondered if this was a good idea or not. It was too late to back down now because Billings was on his way to the visiting area.

When they sat Billings down on the other side of the glass partition, Jake picked up the telephone and said, "Thank you for agreeing to see me. I guess you know who I am."

"Yeah. You are that FBI man who put my daughter in prison."

"Yes. I regret that, but you are the one who set her up and made the case against her so you would not have to go to prison.   I am always sorry when innocent people get hurt. You are not innocent so I have no sympathy for you. You were ultimately responsible for my wife getting shot."

"That John Wesley Williams could not do anything right. He botched it with you on two different occasions. He also got obsessed with getting his money back from you."

"It was actually your money and no one knows for sure I have it, but that does not matter. You are where you belong and John Wesley is out of the picture. I just wanted to tell you in person that if you ever bother my family or me again, I will see to it that your stay in prison is cut very short.   There are several people in here who would be willing to do me a favor because of the way I helped them when they were arrested. They would not have any problem at all bringing your prison stay to a quick end. They do not think much of people who do in their own daughter. If you are ever eligible for a parole hearing I will be there and will do everything I can to make sure you rot in this prison."

Without giving Billings a chance to answer or make any other remarks, Jake hung up the phone and turned and walked out of the visiting area, leaving Billings with the phone in his hand. Jake was not pleased with himself for making threats and he knew that he ought to forgive him, but at the moment it was still all too fresh for him to do that. He also felt that Billings took what he said to heart and would not bother him or his family any more.

CHAPTER 36

THE LAST WORD

WEDNESDAY, DECEMBER 31, 2003

Jake and Barbara had finally worked out some time together and were enjoying the beautiful solitude of winter in the Blue Ridge Mountains. She had been on one of her afternoon runs and had picked up the mail on the way back to the cabin.

As she entered the cabin she said to Jake, "I picked up the mail. Excuse me for reading your mail, but you got the strangest postcard. It was from the Cayman Islands and all it said was, 'This is the closest I will get to my money.' Who in the world would send that and what does it mean?"

"It was from and old friend and it is just an inside joke. I might explain it to you someday if you will be a good girl."

The end?

www.ingramcontent.com/pod-product-compliance
Lightning Source LLC
Chambersburg PA
CBHW071849220626
47052CB00002B/30